# THE TOMBSTONE

# THE TOMBSTONE

*by*
## Will Brennan

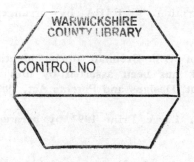

## Dales Large Print Books
### Long Preston, North Yorkshire, England.

British Library Cataloguing in Publication Data.

---

Brennan, Will
   The tombstone.

A catalogue record for this book is
available from the British Library

ISBN 1-85389-771-X pbk

First published in Great Britain by Robert Hale Ltd., 1996

Cover illustration © FABA by arrangement with Norma
Editorial

The right of Will Brennan to be identified as the author
of this work has been asserted by him in accordance with
the Copyright, Designs and Patents Act, 1988

Published in Large Print 1997 by arrangement with Robert
Hale Ltd.

Dales Large Print is an imprint of
Library Magna Books Ltd.
Printed and bound in Great Britain by
T.J. International Ltd., Cornwall, PL28 8RW.

# THE TOMBSTONE

...dale had been built on Shoshoni ...ground, which meant nothing to ...abitants until the day a half-breed ...oni arrived in town. He demanded ...ensation for the land and for the ...er of an old Shoshoni spokesman ...His Horse Is Black. From that ...Marshal Arnold Boyle and the ...ed unimaginable difficulties. Lead ...gan to fly, but in the midst of all ...moke no one was prepared for the ...aftermath.

0135735027

# 1

## Martindale

It was said of Martindale that every notorious person beginning with Liver-Eating Johnson had either lived in Martindale or had passed through.

It was a fact that the town had begun as a log fort where buffalo hunters manned the catwalks when irate tribesmen had attacked over the indiscriminate slaughter of bisons—for the hides only, leaving the meat to rot.

But, by the time the log huts and the fort had been demolished, to make way for a brick bank, a huge emporium, a livery and trading barn, a wagon works operated in conjunction with a smithy, even an apothecary shop beside the saddle and harness works, Martindale's wild and lawless past survived only in the memories of a few old men, mostly crippled up with foggy minds whose reason for existing was now limited to Harney's saloon and benches in the sun.

Along with frontier respectability came the law enforced by a large, powerfully built man with a droopy dragoon moustache named Arnold Boyle. It was said Marshal Boyle could cull wildcats barehanded and if appearance made that seem possible, the lawman's disposition clinched it. He was widely respected, which was not the same as being widely liked. He maintained law and order with ham-sized fists and a blue-black Colt with beautifully carved walnut grips, and upon the rare occasions when it was necessary, with a sawed-off scattergun loaded with lead slugs.

Arnold Boyle was a widower, a widely known fact, but when and how his wife had died no one knew, nor was local curiosity likely to be enlightened; Marshal Boyle rarely talked about himself or his past, which was fine with merchants, roundabout ranchers and the cranky wisp of a shrivelled prune who operated the local stage company, a single man in his late fifties named Jake Miller.

Vestiges of Martindale's lurid past occasionally surfaced and were largely ignored. Once, a few years back when the telegraph people were surveying for the line and during the process of digging post holes, they turned up the shallow grave of a fully attired 'breed Indian in smoke-tans with weapons, medicine rattles and fleshing knife in an elaborately beaded sheath. The old-timers, whose foggy memories precluded recalling what they'd had for breakfast, had no difficulty in identifying the remains as one Shoshoni spokesman called His Horse Is Black, who had disappeared after laying claim by right of heritage to the land where Martindale now stood.

That he had been obviously buried in haste with all his regalia was, or so the old gaffers said, a reliable indication that whites not Indians had interred him. Indians, they said, did not bury their tribesmen with weapons, never with a revolver and a rifle, things by which hostiles set considerable store because they were hard to acquire, harder in fact to acquire than a herd of stolen horses.

The local minister, a man with pale eyes and a square jaw, had tried successfully to solicit funds for a decent reburial and when that had failed had taken it upon himself to move the remains to the church cemetery and reinter them, which occasioned considerable outrage because without question His Horse Is Black was not a Christian and until the reinterment Martindale's cemetery had contained only Christians.

But, inevitably, that indignation faded as time passed. People had livings to make, chores to do, children to mind and families to provide for. But not everyone forgot what was considered locally to be a sacrilege, and the result was that the preacher's congregation dwindled to less than half its normal Sunday attendance.

But, as the minister told Marshal Boyle, who was an irreligious individual, it was the least folks could do since obviously

10

His Horse Is Black had been murdered. The evidence was clear even after so many years. The back of the Indian's skull had been crushed by a powerful blow from behind.

Arnold Boyle avoided taking sides in what he considered a matter between church-goers and their preacher. That the spokesman had been murdered—well—according to the old gaffers that had happened about twenty years ago and Arnold Boyle felt no obligation to delve further because, in that length of time whoever had killed the Shoshoni was probably also dead. And there was the matter of current law enforcement which occupied most of his time.

The telegraph people had made a sashay around the grave, had set their poles and strung their wire to the telegraph office on the west side of Main Street north of the harness works. The operator of the telegraph office was a stooped man addicted to dark sunshades and elegant sleeve garters by the name of Ulysses S.Beaver. Like Marshal Boyle and a few others the telegrapher was not a church-goer, neither was he concerned about an Indian who had been dead long before Ulysses S.Beaver arrived in Martindale.

Clancy Harney, proprietor of the Horse-man's Rest Saloon & Card Room, was another only mildly interested individual. Clancy, with a gut that could be the envy of a pregnant woman, very little grey hair, who was addicted to strong cigars and also wore elegant sleeve garters, shrugged off the matter of a heathen being buried in the local cemetery. Like other causes of local indignation this one would pass when something else arrived to take its place.

An old screwt called Abner Something-or-other, one of the residents of a dilapidated one-time hotel at the lower end of town, which had been abandoned—only the Lord knew why—ten years earlier, was leaning on Clancy's bar savouring a straight whiskey when the topic of the reburial came up. He said he remembered His Horse Is Black very well, that he had been headman, called a spokesman, for a band of Shoshoni who had been forced on to reservations over

12

the spokesman's indignant and eloquent appeals and condemnations.

He said His Horse Is Black even hired a fee-lawyer from back East when he laid claim to the ground Martindale stood on and that with the disappearance of the spokesman the fee-lawyer had returned easterly after which the army arrived to drive the Indians to a distant reservation.

Inevitably someone in the saloon asked what had happened to His Horse Is Black and the old gaffer replied that no one knew, he just did not arrive back at his rancheria after visiting town. Then the old man, tall, bony and sly-eyed, made a humourless smile as he added a little more to what he had just said.

'The In'ians said white men murdered the spokesman. Whites said Indians done it. The fee-lawyer seemed to figure the disappearance a warning and skedaddled back where he come from.'

Clancy had heard the story many times. After the discovery of the bronco's grave not far north of town, a short distance east of the stage road, he had a question for the old scarecrow.

'Did the In'ians bury their dead close to a town?'

Abner gave the saloonman a sly look before replying. 'No sir. They hid their dead in the mountains, sometimes in caves, sometimes on burial platforms. That question was asked back then.' The sly look lingered. 'Old man Martindale who give his name to the town, had been an In'ian fighter most of his life. He told me whites killed the In'ian one night and that's why he just upped and disappeared. If Jess Martindale had been alive when they found the grave he would have said whoever killed him buried him in a hurry.'

The saloon became quiet. Even the saloonman became occupied wiping his bar-top with a moist cloth.

Marshal Boyle was drawn into the mystery when Abner's recitation at the saloon was brought to his attention by the minister. His reaction was what could have been expected. He told the preacher: except for it being a mystery which would likely never be solved; there were a lot of unmarked graves, even Joseph Smith, who founded the Mormon sect, had been shot and to this day no one knew what became of his body. 'Murder pure an' simple but long time ago. Like this In'ian, it happened too long ago. Nowadays we got other problems, all kinds of 'em. Diggin' up the Shoshoni was no good, Preacher. Reburyin' him in the local grave yard stirred up somethin' that happened long ago an' is best forgotten. Your meddlin' just stirred it up all over again.'

The minister, whose pale eyes never wavered, told Arnold Boyle that 'Murder will out, Marshal,' and left the jailhouse.

Marshal Boyle sighed, groped in a drawer for his bottle, returned it slightly depleted and wagged his head. In time this business would die. As far as he was concerned the sooner the better.

The preacher, whose name was Enoch Severn, did something a few weeks later that stirred things up all over again. He made a fine upright tombstone and placed it over the grave of His Horse Is Black. It

15

did not help matters that the grave was close to the ornamental steel fence around the graveyard at the entrance; that was bad enough, but he had incised a Christian cross at the top of the cenotaph and below it had carefully chiselled a legend stating this was the final resting place of Shoshoni His Horse Is Black. In the place ordinarily reserved for dates of birth and death, because the minister knew neither, he had chiselled one word—'Murdered'—and beside it what seemed to be about the month and year.

Even the unusual occurrence of a stage robbery up north, between Martindale and a place called Vermillion, did not interfere with local outrage. The Ladies Altar Society of Preacher Severn's Methodist Church located at the extreme north end of the town, the only white-painted building in Martindale, erupted indignantly. Andrew Sears, the blacksmith, said the ladies had raised hell and popped it up.

Marshal Boyle, who had ridden to the scene of the stage robbery and only returned after the café was closed for the night, cared for his horse behind the jailhouse, went around front, unlocked the door and crossed to the ceiling wire from which hung the lamp. He got the wick set where he wanted it and turned to shed his hat behind the desk. Until then he had no idea a man had followed him into the jailhouse.

The marshal nodded, went to his desk, dropped down and said, 'The first highway robbery since I been here an' it had to happen so far northward I couldn't get back before the café closed.'

The other man, legs pushed out, hat back, grinned. He was younger than the town marshal and was shy about sixty pounds of being as hefty.

He had dark hair and eyes, even features, and a wide mouth that quickened upwards at the corners. He was dressed as a rangeman except for one thing: mostly, rangemen who wore belt guns had the grips that came with the weapons. The stranger's weapon had ivory grips.

Boyle said, 'I'll fire up the stove,' and arose to cross the room to the kindling box. The visitor said nothing, just watched. When the stove was popping and the lawman had returned to his desk the stranger spoke for the first time.

'Nice town.'

Marshal Boyle nodded. 'I like it, plenty of shade, the water's good, folks that got stores do right well. By any chance you figurin' on settlin' in an' startin' a business?'

The stranger continued to wear his relaxed small smile as he shook his head and spoke. 'I got no trade, Marshal, except drivin' stage and workin' as a helper at a smithy. I worked cattle and broke horses. That's about the size of it.'

Boyle nodded. What the dark-eyed man said fitted most men of the Nevada's livestock country. 'The smith might put you on,' he told the younger man and got a slightly negative wag of the stranger's head.

'I didn't come here to find work, Marshal. I made a little money in the Territory. Just thought I'd move around this summer. By the way, I was ridin' a rim up north when that stage got stopped. I was some distance off and the light wasn't real good. It was close to sundown. I saw everythin' that happened but couldn't make out much about the fellers who robbed it, except that there was two of 'em an' one rode a big *grulla* horse.'

Boyle considered the younger, lithe, dark-eyed man. 'Which way did they go?'

'North. I passed a town called Vermillion some miles upcountry. That was the direction they took. You have a telegraph?'

'Yes. But Vermillion don't. The line come south-east through the mountains an' bypassed Vermillion. You didn't get a look at the highwaymen?'

'No. Just that there was two an' one rode a big *grulla* horse. Mostly, their backs was to me. What did they get?'

'I don't know yet. The corralyard's locked up for the night but in the mornin' I'll hear about it. The stage company's manager here has a disposition like a bear with a sore behind. I'll hear about it in the mornin'.' Marshal Boyle hesitated a moment before saying, 'You figure to stay

19

around a day or two, do you? I didn't catch your name.'

'The name's Hugh Black. I can lie over for a spell.'

'I'd take it kindly. So would the screwt that runs the stages. You know where the hotel is?'

Hugh Black nodded and arose. 'See you in the mornin', Marshal.'

The big man leaned back at his desk after the stranger had departed. If the highwaymen went towards Vermillion, which was a good day and a half's ride from Martindale, he could look forward to going up there with a couple of blank warrants.

Vermillion was across the hills. It was more a mining town than a cattle town. He knew the local lawman up there only passingly.

If the highwaymen had stopped at Vermillion, fine, but if they hadn't, had simply passed the place continuing northward—or easterly, westerly or even southerly—Marshal Boyle would make the ride to Vermillion for nothing. However, he had to go and in a slightly less than enthusiastic frame of mind he locked up for the night, went over to Clancy's place for a nightcap and heard something interesting. A rider who worked for one of the outlying ranches had told Clancy he'd seen a pair of horsemen riding due west in a high lope, and after learning about the stage robbery, was willing to bet he had seen the highwaymen.

Marshal Boyle groaned inwardly. Should he take a chance and ride westerly in the hope that that hired rider had actually seen the outlaws, or should he go up to Vermillion?

He downed his nightcap, dropped a coin beside the sticky little glass and headed for his room at the hotel, which was actually a rooming-house.

He would go north to Vermillion.

# 2

## Getting known

Mostly, Nevada did not get much rain, even in springtime. For that matter Nevada was largely desert, barren hills and land that was worthless except for livestock because of the lack of rainfall.

But it had minerals in abundance. Mines prospered, miners always had employment, their towns, different from the livestock settlements tended more towards creature comforts. In Vermillion, for example, there was a milliner, a physician, and four saloons; the largest and most patronized called itself a tavern, as though that lent it more respectability than saloons had.

There was an awful lot of Nevada where crows flying over had to pack their food and where scorpions, snakes and buzzards existed by devouring one another. A slow jack-rabbit in Nevada did not stand a chance.

Clancy Harney, proprietor of the Horseman's Rest in Martindale had settled first up in Vermillion, had owned a saloon up there for six years, and had sold out because mining and miners were things he did not care for. Clancy had been raised hard in Nebraska. He had left as soon as he had two cartwheels to rub together, but having matured in livestock country, mines and miners were not just alien to him, they spoke a language that took him six years to completely understand.

Clancy, who hadn't been able to lean across his bar for years because of his *ponzas*, had several high stools between the back-bar mirror and bottles and the counter where he could perch when he cared to.

He perched on one of those high stools the morning Marshal Boyle left town riding north shortly before daybreak, and was still perched there reading an old newspaper someone had abandoned, when an easy-moving rangeman with dark eyes crossed

23

to the bar which allowed Clancy time to see the elegant six-gun the stranger wore.

He stashed the newspaper, slid off the stool and smiled. It was early for drinking, but Clancy Harney sold liquor not watches.

The lithe stranger asked for beer and while Clancy was drawing it off he leaned on the counter looking around. When the glass arrived the stranger said, 'Looks like you don't get much business early mornings.'

That was a fact. 'Not right after breakfast, unless it's some of them old men who live on the edge of town. Some of them make it through the day with a jolt or two instead of food.'

'You know 'em, do you?'

Clancy nodded. He dispensed leavings which he poured into a gallon jug and sold to the old men for five cents a jolt glass. 'I know 'em. I used to know all of 'em but they die off.'

'How about an old man named Abner Halt?'

'Sure do. Folks dug up an old In'ian.

He'd been buried a long time but ol' Abner knew his name an' all about him. I don't think anyone else did.'

The stranger half-emptied his beer glass, paid up and asked where Abner lived. Clancy scooped up the coin while replying.

'There's an old abandoned hotel at the lower end of town. Those old men live in there like rats in a burrow. That used to be where hide-hunters lived. I don't have no idea who owned it but it was there when the hide-hunters drifted off one an' two at a time until it was empty. No one ever claimed the old building.'

The stranger thanked Clancy, when out front, down as far as the emporium and sat on a bench while he rolled, lighted and smoked a cigarette.

The clerk came out to hang collars and harness hames on nails. He smiled and the stranger smiled back. The clerk wore his hair parted in the middle and slicked down on both sides. He wore plain black cloth sleeve protectors. He sat down on the stranger's bench and said, 'Goin' to be a nice day.'

The stranger smiled and killed his quirley. 'For a fact. How's business?'

'Good. Mister Hammond's got the only general store for miles in all directions.'

The stranger said, 'Hammond? Arthur Hammond?'

'Yes sir, that's him. He started the store thirty years ago. Back then his business was mostly tinned goods an' horseshoes. He traded a lot with In'ians.' The clerk arose. 'Well, nice talkin' to you. I got to get back inside.'

Directly opposite the emporium was the jailhouse, one of the few structures along Main Street which had both a sod roof and log walls. It was ugly in a quaint way. Most other buildings in Martindale had peaked, wooden roofs and planed board siding.

Behind the jailhouse was a pole corral and a shed where lawmen over the years had kept horses.

The abandoned hotel at the southerly end of town had fir logs for its foundation instead of rocks. Fir was strong but the best fir heart-wood eventually rotted. With the old hotel this was responsible for a noticeable list to the building, the upper floor seemed to list the most.

It had a number of small rooms, rather like a rabbit warren. The old men who lived down there had two communal stoves but only the toughest of the residents could still go out for wood. The result was that pneumonia in bitter winters accounted for more deaths than whiskey did. Whiskey and malnutrition.

The stranger found Abner Holt on the first floor and was invited in. The room was draped with grey, freshly washed clothing suspended from three cast-aside old lariats. Abner made no apologies. He offered the stranger coffee whose strength was maintained by adding a fistful of ground beans to what was already in the speckleware pot.

The stranger declined with thanks. When old Abner sat opposite the stranger, leaning so that drying drawers would not touch him, the stranger introduced himself. 'My name is Hugh Black. I never been in this country before.'

Abner made a gummer's grin. 'If you

figure to work as a rangeman, friend, there's some big outfits, an' early spring is when they hire on.'

Hugh Black nodded. 'Maybe I'll nosy around. I just come to Martindale a day or so ago. I guess I timed it wrong. A stage was robbed an' folks are roiled up.'

'Good reason, friend. Ain't been a stage robbed around Martindale in more years than I like to recollect.'

The dark-eyed, soft-speaking, lithe younger man said, 'I heard about an In'ian bein' dug up an' maybe—'

'That,' Abner interjected, 'was months back.' He grinned, showing wet gums. 'The preacher got in hot water for reburyin' the old bronco in the church cemetery, which was bad enough, seein' as how the In'ian was a heathen, but he set up a tall tombstone over the grave.'

'Folks didn't like that either?'

'Nope, they sure didn't.'

'Who was the old In'ian?'

'Feller called His Horse Is Black.'

'Did you know him?'

'Yes, knew him right well. His band had

a rancheria back in the mountains.'

'How did he die?'

'That's the mystery, friend. He was face-down-dead when they dug him up beside the road north of town. I'd guess he'd been put there about twenty years ago. I doubt if there's more 'n a handful of folks still around who remember that. There'll be some, like the man who owns the general store, some cowmen most likely, maybe the blacksmith, but mostly folks who was around then have died or left the country.'

Hugh Black got the discussion back to the death. 'I heard he was buried in a shallow grave with his guns.'

Abner nodded. 'I heard that too. In fact he was buried in his smoke-tans, which they only wore on real special occasions.' Abner hung fire a moment gazing over the visitor's head. 'The preacher's taken him up an' reburied him like I told you. He might know how he died.' Abner's gaze dropped to the younger man's face, 'Mister Black, we're talkin' about somethin' that's most likely not good to talk about.'

'Why? It happened twenty years ago and—'

Abner's gaze was fixed on his visitor when he interrupted to say, 'There's talk about how the In'ian died.'

'Murdered?'

Abner, who had been getting uncomfortable the longer this conversation went on, arose, turned his back on Hugh Black and ran his fingers over his drying laundry. 'Talk to Preacher Severn.'

Hugh Black arose, slapped Abner lightly on the shoulder and said, 'I'm obliged, Mister Holt,' and departed leaving Abner gazing after him with squinted eyes. The stranger hadn't asked Abner's last name and Abner had not mentioned it.

Martindale's respectability, like most villages and towns west of the Big Muddy was to some extent based on its church and the congregation. On Sundays the parishoners were mostly women and youngsters. Men attended but never in large numbers. Enoch Severn had formed an opinion about that long ago. The men who came to church were invariably married men whose wives used whatever guile was necessary to get them there.

Preacher Severn was an individual to whom right was right and wrong was wrong. There were few grey areas but at his age after something like twenty-five years preaching the Gospel, he had grudgingly come to slightly expand his tolerance—if not his understanding—of the grey areas.

He took Hugh Black into his garden behind the rectory, offered him lemonade which the dark-eyed younger man declined, and sat in shade beneath a huge, unkempt old sycamore tree. He spoke of his reburied Indian without hesitation, why he had defied local conviction about a nonbeliever being buried among believers, was simply because death is a leveller. Judgement may be something different, but on earth the dead departed deserved a decent burial, not some shallow trench made and covered furtively with no words of commendation said over the grave.

Hugh Black relaxed in his old chair, tipped his hat back, shoved out his legs and faintly nodded before he asked a question which drove the minister into a moment of silence, but eventually he said, 'It had to be murder, didn't it? His skull was smashed from in back. His weapons hadn't been fired, his knife was in its sheath.' Enoch Severn studied the visitor. 'Would you like to see the weapons?'

'You didn't bury them with him?'

'No. Where he went they don't need or use weapons. He went to a peaceful and tranquil place.'

'An In'ian in your heaven, Mister Severn?'

The minister leaned forward clasping his hands. 'My friend, when you cut yourself is your blood red?'

'Yes.'

'And so is mine.'

Hugh Black regarded the minister steadily for a moment before asking another question. 'Were you around when he was killed?'

'No. I didn't hear the rumours until the telegraph people accidentally dug him up.'

'But you've heard talk, rumours?'

'Never until he was dug up,' the minister said, and bored his visitor with a look. 'Mister, I expect folks could say I'm takin' this too much to heart. I know they think I did wrong buryin' him in the local cemetery, but it's bothered me since they dug him up. For one thing, I've served in many places where gossip and rumours were the breath of life to folks. But in Martindale, after the old Indian was found it's like an oath of silence had come over people. Even the marshal don't want to talk about the human-being I reburied. When I bring up the subject folk walk away or change the subject. Not all of 'em, mind you, but the others stare right through me, an' one, Clancy Harney, who owns the saloon opposite the bank—took me aside out front of the emporium and told me to leave sleepin' dogs lie.'

Hugh Black considered the toes of his scuffed boots before saying, 'It might be good advice, Reverend.'

Severn inclined his head. 'For a fact my Sunday services now have about half the folks show up as before.'

33

Hugh Black slowly arose. 'I expect most things that happened that long ago might as well be forgotten.'

Enoch Severn escorted his visitor around front and down to the little picket gate which he held aside for Hugh Black to pass through. The last thing he said was: '"Vengeance is mine, saith the Lord, an' I shall repay".'

Black looked straight at the minister when he replied to that quotation from Scriptures. 'Yes indeed. An' the Lord works in mysterious ways, Mister Severn; sometimes I expect He appoints us human-beings to do His work—to do His vengeance.'

A dog fight erupted in the middle of the road down in front of the saloon. No one tried to stop it until a man wearing an apron emerged from the harness shop and broke it up.

Hugh Black watched onlookers drift away and the harness-maker return to his shop. Black kept to the west plankwalk and passed most businesses until he reached the smithy where an older man who was sinewy rather than muscular was buckling on his farrier's apron and studying a 1,400 pound draft horse cross-tied between his forge and anvil.

When Hugh Black walked in, the smith nodded, went to a hanging bucket, drank a dipperful of water then turned to say, 'You got an animal needs shoein'?'

Hugh Black's reply was indecisive. 'In a week or so.'

The smith went to the right shoulder of the large horse, ran his hand from withers to fetlock and tugged. The big horse lifted his foot. The smith smoothed its hoof clean with a rough textured hand and spoke over his shoulder. 'They let 'em go until the last minute. Look at this, hoof's danged near overgrown the shoe.'

Hugh Black looked and moved clear. 'You got a blank that size?'

The smith shook his head. 'Nope. I got to make 'em. That foot's as big as a dinner plate.' He dropped the hoof, moved toward his forge, pitched in pine kindling, blew on it until a flame appeared then worked the bellows, which made noise. He considered his visitor. 'You ever do shoein'?'

'Cowboy shoeing.'

The smith nodded curtly. In his opinion cowboy horseshoers caused more lame animals than barbed wire cuts.

Hugh Black looked for a place to sit that wasn't layered with soot and the blacksmith smiled and pointed to a cubbyhole office where Hugh found a chair and brought it forth to sit on as he raised his voice above the bellows to say, 'Nice town.'

'You just come in?'

'Day or two ago. I was comin' south on a ridge an' saw that stage get robbed.'

The smith stopped pumping. 'Who was he?'

'There was two of 'em. I was on a rim with daylight fadin'. All I saw was the robbery an' them boys ride north. One of 'e ridin' a fair-sized blue horse.'

'Did you tell this to the marshal?'

'Yesterday evening.'

The smith took another drink from the hanging bucket, faced around and wiped his chin. 'This here big horse belongs to the stage company. They brought him in this mornin'. Feller who's boss up there was mad about that robbery.' The smith resumed pumping the bellows and had to raise his voice as he said, 'He's always mad about somethin'. Good thing he ain't married. Any woman worth her salt would have blown his head off long ago.'

Hugh Black said, 'What's his name?'

'Jake Miller.' The smith moved to place a length of steel into the cherry-red coals of his forge. When he had turned it several times before removing it from the coals to shape it on the anvil, the dark-eyed man was gone. He paid little heed to that. He had to shape the steel before it cooled.

The music of his working the anvil reached all the way north to the saloon where Clancy was polishing glasses and admiring himself in the back-bar mirror when the dark-eyed stranger walked in, smiled, and asked for beer. Clancy drew it off, placed it in front of his only patron and would have returned to polishing glasses if the beer-drinker hadn't asked a peculiar question. 'You been in Martindale twenty years, have you?'

Clancy hadn't and shook his head.

The beer-drinker did not touch the glass. He leaned with both hands around it still smiling. 'How about the blacksmith; he been here that long.'

Clancy nodded.

'An' the feller who owns the general store?'

'Yes.'

'How about the man who bosses for the stage company?'

Clancy's brows drew together slightly. 'He arrived with the livestock and rigs. That was a long time ago. It was rough country back then, so they've told me. Are you goin' to maybe write a book?'

Hugh Black half drained the glass before answering. 'I'm footloose an' I like what I've seen so far. Would you say Martindale's a decent place for a man to settle in?'

Clancy's brow cleared. He nodded. 'Kind of hot come summer, an' exceptin' local business and the ranches, there's not

38

much opportunity. You could hire on with a cow outfit. This time of year they're hirin'.'

Black considered what remained in his glass as he said, 'I thought about that.'

Clancy, feeling on solid ground with this turn of their conversation added a little more. 'The Martindale country is one of them places where you either work for someone or come here with plenty of money, because partner, you won't make any on your own. You ever tend bar?'

'No sir, I never did.'

Clancy sighed. He had a married son out in San Francisco and had wanted to visit him, which he could not do without closing the saloon and that would not only cost him money, it would alienate his customers.

'Would you be interested in learnin' the trade?' he asked

Hugh Black's amiable smile surfaced. 'Maybe, but not for a while. I figure to ride around, meet folks, figure whether this is where I want to settle in.'

Outside those two dogs were at it again

and this time no one stopped them. Hugh went past the spindle doors, watched, saw the smaller dog getting pretty badly chewed up and walked through the onlookers to the roadway, caught hold of the larger dog by the scruff of his neck and the back, yanked him chest high, faced the onlookers and hurled him at them. People scattered. A large burly, bearded man attired in a checkered shirt stepped off the plankwalk. 'Let 'em finish it,' he told Hugh as he walked steadily toward the lighter, more lithe man. 'I don't take kindly to no son of a bitch throwin' my dog around.'

People seemed to take root on both sides of the roadway. Clancy was in his doorway, other merchants came out to watch. The bearded man's features were nearly hidden by whiskers but there was no mistaking his eyes, they were fixed and menacing.

Hugh Black let the burly man get within several feet of him before saying, 'That's far enough.'

The burly man continued his march. He was close enough to ball both fists when Hugh sprang ahead, struck him in the mouth and twisted sideways as the burly man snarled and lunged.

The second strike caught the bearded man under the ear. He went down like a pole-axed steer. There was not a sound. Hugh looked for the small dog but it had fled. He leaned, removed the bearded man's holstered Colt, shucked it empty and dropped it. He considered the onlookers. 'This feller belong to any of you?'

The silence was total.

'Throw some water over him,' Hugh said. 'Tell him I'll be at the livery barn if he wants to try again.'

A few murmurs went among the spectators as they watched Hugh Black stay in the centre of the roadway until he was abreast of the barn, then turned toward the doorless wide opening where the blacksmith and the liveryman were standing. He nodded and walked past, all the way to the stall where his horse stood hip-shot and replete.

The blacksmith looked at the liveryman. 'He was in my shop earlier.'

'Who is he?'

'Damned if I know, but when the marshal gets back he'll want to know.'

'Where is he?' the liveryman asked. 'He ought to be in town.'

The smith was heading for his own shop when he replied. 'Damned if I know.'

# 3

## An Exasperated Lawman

Marshal Boyle's return was uneventful; he did not reach Martindale until close to midnight. Even the rooming house was locked up for the night; he had to jimmy a warped window to get into his room. He hadn't been in a good frame of mind since being told up in Vermillion that as far as the local law knew no stranger had ridden in on a *grulla* horse, but Marshal Boyle was welcome to ask round, which he had done without success. This left him with no alternative but to make the long ride back to Martindale.

Both he and his horse were tired by the time they reached Martindale and Marshal Boyle slept until after sun-up, awakened, went out back to the wash house, cleaned up and went over to the café looking unfriendly and feeling that way.

Andy Sears was finishing his second cup of coffee when Boyle eased down at the counter, growled his order and looked around to nod. The blacksmith said, 'Do any good up north?'

Boyle shook his head and concentrated on the mug of black java the caféman placed before him. Sears considered the marshal's profile and said no more.

The jailhouse's log walls prevented all but the loudest sounds to penetrate. They also provided insulation against fierce summer heat and, if the door was ajar, the scents of springtime permeated an otherwise gloomy, poorly lighted and stale-smelling old structure.

The big man was relaxing at his desk when a wisp of an older man walked in and began a harangue about someone sicking a big dog on his little bitch, and he wanted action.

'It's a gawddamned shame when a pup can't go down the road without some sonbitch turnin' a fightin' dog on it. She's on her blanket scairt to move, won't eat and shivers all the time. She got bit real bad.'

Marshal Boyle nodded toward a chair. He had known the corralyard boss for years, had encountered his temper many times and today, still weary after his ride up north and back without a single tangible result, he bluntly said, 'How much did them highwaymen make off with, Jake?'

'An' that's another thing,' the older man said. 'Where was you yestiddy when I went lookin' for you? Out somewhere smellin' flowers? Your job is to—'

'How much, Jake!'

'Three hunnert dollars off the whip an' his passengers.'

'No mail sacks, no bank money?'

The wispy old man glared. 'It's got to be bullion or a shipment of new money for the bank, does it?'

Boyle's anger was stirring. He was not by nature a compliant individual and, although he had learned over the years to tolerate the stager's crankiness, this particular day with his tailbone still aching from all the fruitless saddle-backing, he was not ready to accommodate what he was hearing, so he leaned on the desk, large hands clasped as he said, 'Is your pup goin' to make it?'

Jake Miller was caught unprepared for the abrupt switch in their conversation and stared before replying. 'She'll make it. But except for that newcomer called Hugh Something-or-other, she would have been bit to death.'

Marshal Boyle regarded the smaller and older man a moment before saying, 'Hugh?'

'Dark-eyed feller, maybe in his thirties, he's been around a spell. He ain't exactly a stranger. Clancy said he'd heard this feller seen the stage robbery. I figure to talk to him. Passengers gettin' robbed on our coaches won't set well with the company in Denver.'

Marshal Boyle eased back. He knew which man Jake Miller had mentioned. 'He broke up the dog fight?'

Jake snorted. 'More'n that, he yanked the fightin' dog off my pup by the scruff an' when the feller who owns the dog started to make trouble, this stranger knocked him senseless, right in the middle of the road.' The cranky old man arose and turned to depart, but he had one last jibe to pronounce. 'That's the kind of lawman Martindale needs, not someone who rides out to smell the damned flowers!'

Marshal Boyle reflected on what the stager had said and went over to the emporium for a sack of Durham before going up to the saloon. The large, heavy proprietor was in conversation with the dark-eyed stranger who had told Marshal Boyle of witnessing the stage robbery.

Hammond was portly, thin-lipped with dark eyes and skimpy grey thatch. He was married, his only child, a son, was back in Chicago and rarely visited Martindale. It was said of Arthur Hammond he had acquired wealth any way he could. That description had been put on him years earlier and still stuck. That he was one of the founders of Martindale's bank did little to add to Hammond's popularity as a manipulator and a money-man.

What Marshal Boyle noticed from down

by the clerk's station near the cash drawer, was that while he could not see Hugh Black's face, by looking over Black's shoulder he could see Hammond's face and the portly man with the big gold chain across his middle did not look as though he was enjoying their conversation.

Nor was he, but until Hugh Black had departed and he saw Arnold Boyle standing near the door did the lawman get a scrap of information that troubled him.

Hammond said, 'Do you know that feller I was talkin' to Marshal?'

'Well, I know who he is. Come to town a few days back. He saw the stage robbery from a ridge, came in to tell me what he saw. What about him, Mister Hammond?'

'I'm not sure. I'll let you know if a suspicion I got is right in a day or two.'

'Is he a fugitive?' the marshal asked.

Hammond's reply was softly given. 'I don't know about that. I'll look you up in a few days.'

Boyle watched the portly man leave the store, paid for his purchase and also left.

On his stroll in the direction of Clancy's watering hole he did some reflecting. He had known Mister Hammond since the first day he'd ridden into Martindale. During that lengthy acquaintanceship he had never seen the emporium owner look seriously upset until today, and whatever it was, that Hugh Black individual was involved.

Clancy had three bearded and brawny teamsters at his bar. Until he had satisfied them he could not go down to where the marshal was waiting. On the way he got a bottle and jolt glass but the marshal pushed them aside as he said, 'Clancy, what do you know about that Hugh Black feller?'

The saloonman's eyes widened. 'Not much. He's been in here a few times. Is he wanted?'

Marshal Boyle ignored the question. 'When he's in here what does he talk about?'

'Nothin' much. Said he liked Martindale and figures he might settle here. Is he an outlaw?' Again the marshal avoided an answer. He left the saloonman gazing after

49

him until the freighters growled for refills, then he hastened back up the bar.

Andy Sears was setting up his rig for sweating new steel tyres on to a wheel off one of the stage coaches when Boyle walked in. He wiped both hands on an oily cloth as he faced the marshal.

Boyle rarely wasted words. He asked what the blacksmith knew about Hugh Black and watched Sears's face begin to show wariness.

'He seems like a nice feller, Marshal. I saw him break up that dog fight when old Jake's pup was gettin' the worst of it.'

'What did he talk about, Andy?'

'Talk about? Nothin' in particular. About shoein'; nothin' in particular. Marshal, is he an outlaw?'

As before Boyle ignored the question and departed from the smithy. Andy Sears watched him leave, wearing a puzzled expression. He finally shrugged and turned back to his work.

The harness-maker, a bird-like, wiry, high-strung man had had no association with the dark-eyed stranger but he had seen Black visit with Enoch Severn at the parsonage, so Marshal Boyle went up there. But the preacher had gone to one of the outlying cow outfits in his buggy. Both the horse and rig were gone, so the marshal went over to the telegraph office, but Ulysses S. Beaver did not even know anyone named Hugh Black and he had neither sent nor received any telegraph message for him.

Boyle returned to his office, tossed his hat aside, sat down and rocked back. From what he had learned only one person appeared to be concerned about Hugh Black, and that was Arthur Hammond.

In disgust the marshal went over to the beanery, and the man seated at the counter on his left was Hugh Black.

The dark-eyed man was pleasant but Marshal Boyle was brusque, with no reason except that Mister Hammond had been upset by the dark-eyed man who was becoming an enigma.

They met again, out front of the café where Hugh Black was rolling a smoke. It seemed almost as though he was deliberately waiting out there. He greeted big Marshal Boyle pleasantly. Boyle mumbled and did not smile as he said, 'I heard about you breakin' up the dog-fight.'

Hugh trickled smoke. 'It wasn't a fight, Marshal. That little dog was scairt to death. Do you know when a dog is whipped? When it rolls on to its back exposin' its soft parts. That means it gives up. That fightin' dog tore into the pup's unprotected parts.'

'So you stepped in.'

'I like dogs, Marshal. That fightin' dog would have killed that pup.'

'Do they have dogs where you come from, Mister Black?'

The younger man smiled and trickled smoke. 'Is that how you find out where folks are from, Marshal?'

Boyle reddened. 'All right. Where are you from?'

'Lots of places.'

'Let's narrow it down. Where was you born?'

'In the Territory.'

'In'ian territory? Oklahoma?'

'Yes. Where was you born, Marshal?'

This time when his colour mounted Boyle's glare was unmistakably hostile. Hugh Black dropped his smoke and ground it underfoot without looking away from the big lawman.

Marshal Boyle stepped off the plankwalk and went directly toward his jailhouse. Behind him, Hugh Black watched from an expressionless face.

They did not meet again for three days and during that interim the lawman had had a long talk with the preacher, who was a direct, forthright individual. He told the marshal about his talk under the old sycamore tree with Hugh Black, but the way it sounded to Marshal Boyle was that the preacher had done most of the talking, had spent a half-hour explaining why he had buried that old tomahawk who had been accidentally dug up.

All he said about Hugh Black was that he seemed unwilling to agree with the minister, but he did not disagree with him either.

It was the day following the lawmam's visit with the preacher that he met Hugh Black at the livery barn where Hugh had cross-tied his horse to bathe it and was still out back when Boyle walked in and the liveryman told him where he could find him.

When Boyle appeared in the wide, doorless alleyway opening out back Hugh saw him. He was skiving water off with a bent wooden stick used for that purpose.

The horse was in his prime years, somewhere around seven, eight or nine. He was a breedy animal which gave Marshal Boyle something to open the conversation with. He told Hugh Black he'd seen thoroughbred racehorses that didn't have the build of Black's leggy, muscled-up bay.

Hugh finished the 'towelling' and stood back looking at his animal as he said, 'I got him in a trade over in New Mexico three years ago. I never raced him. We're friends, I don't make money off friends.'

Marshal Boyle leaned in the doorway. 'You figure to maybe settle in around here?'

'Maybe. It's good country, not like the parts of Nevada I rode through to get here.' Hugh faced around. 'I don't think you'n me would ever hitch horses, Marshal.'

'Why wouldn't we?'

'You got mad when I asked where you was born but it was all right for you to ask me that.'

Boyle said, 'I was born in Nebraska not far from Council Bluffs.'

The liveryman appeared to say some freighters were fighting at the saloon. Marshal Boyle left Hugh standing with his wet-shiny horse.

By the time the lawman reached the saloon the fight was over. Clancy had cold-cocked one of the fighters with an ash buggy-spoke kept under the bar for that purpose, and the other two freighters had dragged the unconscious man back to their wagon camp north of town.

Clancy was still holding the spoke when Marshal Boyle pushed past the spindle doors. He gestured. 'Two broke chairs, knocked over two full spittoons.' Clancy wagged his head. 'I'm goin' to nail up a sign, No Freighters Allowed.'

'What was the fight about?' Boyle asked.

'One of 'em swore the other one had said he'd pay for the drinks. The other feller called him a liar. Look at them chairs.'

The marshal left Clancy with his mess, returned to the livery barn but Hugh Black had gone for a ride, the liveryman said, and eyed the marshal askance. 'Somethin' goin' on between you two?'

Marshal Boyle's mood was bleak when he replied. 'You got a long nose,' he said and returned to the jailhouse.

Along towards evening the cranky old stager walked into the marshal's office. Without preliminaries he said, 'That feller who stopped my pup from gettin' killed sewed her up.'

Boyle said, 'When?'

'Fifteen minutes or so ago. He must've done that before. He got some gut from the harness shop an' a crooked needle. I held her an' he done as professional a job as a pill-pusher could've done. Did a real good job. I wanted to pay him an' he just smiled, petted the pup and left. Now, Marshal, that's the kind of folks we need in Martindale.'

Boyle sighed, nodded and after the stager had departed he blew out a big breath and fished for the bottle of popskull he kept in a box under his desk.

That damned stranger was getting to be a problem. He was likely the only person in Martindale that disagreeable old Jake Miller had a good word for.

Black didn't show up at the saloon that evening, but Clancy, who had been told by old Jake Miller what the newcomer had done with his dog, had repeated the story to his customers and when the marshal came by for his nightcap, in a surly mood, and one of the townsmen at the bar said he thought folks should thank the newcomer, Marshal Boyle, with two jolts under his belt, snarled at the suggestion.

'Thank the son of a bitch! He's not here because he likes Martindale!'

A bull-necked cowman arose from his card game. 'Marshal, you ever had a good dog you was fond of?'

'No! In my business a man don't need no dog!'

The cowman looked steadily at the marshal when he said, 'Now me, I've owned dogs I thought more of than fellers like you.'

Boyle turned from the bar. The noisy saloon became totally silent until another man, this one wearing a red plaid shirt, the mark of freighters, broke the hush when he addressed Marshal Boyle. 'That feller's dead right. I've owned mules I thought more of than fellers like you—an overgrown bully with a badge!'

Clancy reached below the bar, straightened up and spoke directly to the freighter. 'Mister, get your butt out of my saloon an' don't you never come back in here.'

The freighter saw the ash spoke, picked up his shot glass and threw it. Clancy ducked. When he rose up from behind the other the freighter was gone, but the cowman who had first confronted Marshal Boyle was still on his feet. Several other patrons stood up.

Clancy leaned to say, 'Marshal, do me

a favour. Leave. I can't get broke chairs fixed. You had your drink, go on up to the hotel an' bed down.'

The big lawman did not move. It wasn't just the jolt of whiskey, Marshal Boyle was a fighting man born and raised. He set his back to the bar, glaring at the standing men facing him along the bar and among the card tables.

The irate cowman spoke again. 'You do a good job at keepin' order, Marshal. Right now you're barkin' up the wrong tree. Clancy gave you some good advice. Don't do anythin' you'll regret, an' the rest of us'll regret.'

Two townsmen came barging through the roadway door, stopped dead still, turned and went back out into the evening. That struck someone funny. The man laughed. That sound did not dispel much of the tension but it helped.

Clancy leaned over again. 'Like the man said, don't do nothin' you'll regret. Two of them gents among the tables is on the town council.'

Marshal Boyle relaxed. He glared at the

standing men, started to say something, thought better of it and stamped out into the dusk.

Clancy shoved the spoke back where it belonged. The cowman who had first called Marshal Boyle came to the bar and gestured. Without hesitation other men came up to the bar where Clancy was as busy as a kitten in a box of shavings setting up bottles and glasses.

Very little was said about the marshal or the tension he had created. He was good at keeping order, no one could deny that.

Clancy was closing up for the night some hours later when Hugh Black walked in. Clancy regarded him stonily, grumbled and went behind the bar to set up a bottle and a glass. He said, 'It's late. I'd like to lock up.'

Hugh nodded, downed his whiskey and blew out a flammable breath, placed a coin beside the glass and said, 'Good night. You're closin' early aren't you?'

Clancy was nettled. 'You see any customers?'

'No. First time I've seen your place empty.'

'If you'd been in here earlier you'd know why there's no customers an' why I want to lock up.'

When Hugh would have spoken Clancy held up a hand. 'Good night, Mister Black!'

# 4

## The Search

Hugh Black bought two bottles of panther piss, took them down to the dilapidated old two-storey building, knocked on Abner Holt's door and was greeted by a whisker-stubbled old stork of a man whose eyes flickered to the bottles first, then to Hugh Black as he stepped aside for the younger man to enter.

This time an ancient tan army blanket was drying on the ropes draped across the room near the stove.

As before, Abner gestured toward the chair and sat himself on an upended little horseshoe keg.

Hugh handed one of the bottles to the old man and placed the other one on a low shelf as he said, 'For your friends.'

Abner held his bottle. 'What do you

want?' he asked, and got a circuitous reply.

'You know this country well?'

'Hell, I'd ought to. I buffler hunted, scouted for In'ians, carried the mail from up north, freighted an' drove stage. I know it. Why?'

'Them In'ians that used to live here, do you know where they had their rancheria?'

'Sure I know that. I told you, I was friends with the one they dug up. Rode up there lots of times. Even hunted with 'em.'

'Can you tell me how to find the place?' Black asked.

Abner considered the whiskey bottle, read the label with obvious effort and looked up. 'Where'd you get this? Do you know what it is? Genuwine bonded whiskey. Clancy don't even own liquor like this.'

Black ignored that statement. 'Can you tell me how to find the old rancheria?'

Abner held the bottle between his knees as he said, 'Why? Nothin' up there but some old fire rings, maybe some wolf-dug graves.'

'When was the last time you was up

there?' Black asked.

Abner squinted and made a slow reply. 'I'd say maybe six, eight years back. Went pot-huntin'. Dang near got a big elk but he outsmarted me. Did you know folks say elks is as smart as men?'

Hugh leaned forward. 'How can I find the rancheria?'

Abner wagged his head. This young fellow was as pig-headed as a brindle bull. He started mentioning land marks, rocks, blazed trees, several very old trails worn into rock, and ended up saying, 'You'll come to a big meadow. Some folks call 'em parks. Sixty, eighty acres. Lots of pine and fir an' a sweetwater creek cutting right through.' He fell momentarily silent. When he resumed speaking his voice changed, he was reliving old memories. 'They wasn't like the Digger In'ians. They stole horses an' cattle but what the hell, the game was gone. That feller they killed—he could make a man laugh over a busted leg, an' he knew In'ian doctorin' which in them days was better'n we had down here. Mister, if you got a bellyache in what's now Martindale in them days, you died. Just upped and died. Did you know that In'ian they dug up had a wife—a "woman" they called 'em? Didn't know about preachers an' all.'

'Did you know her?' Hugh asked.

Abner nodded. 'Not real well. They'd got touchy about white men bein' around their women.'

'What did she look like?'

'Tall, mister. Tall as her man. Taller'n most women. Her'n the other women stayed apart when I'd ride up to visit. I think she was considerable younger'n her man.' The old man roused himself. 'You goin' up there?'

'Yes.'

'Why?'

'I like the country. If I figure to settle here the more I know the better, eh?'

Abner nodded. 'I expect so... Mister, I thank you for the bottles. My friends'll thank you.' The gaunt old man stood up. 'Every time we meet you talk about In'ians. This time you want to visit where their rancheria used to be. Mister, if you don't mind I'd like to ask why? I know, you like the territory an' figure to maybe settle here. Fine. Now then—why do you really want to go up yonder?'

Hugh Black arose facing the old man. 'Be best if I didn't answer, Mister Holt,' he said extending his hand. The old string-bean's grip was surprisingly strong.

Abner said, 'I'm old and wearin' out, but I didn't live this long not gettin' to know people pretty well. That's all right, Mister Black, you got a reason an' as far as I'm concerned we never had this talk. Be careful up there, lots of bears.'

When Hugh arrived at the livery barn the proprietor was removing fine-harness from a buggy mare. Enoch Severn was standing by. The liveryman barely nodded to Hugh but the minister came around the rig and offered his hand. As they talked the liveryman fumbled and re-fumbled with harness-hooks and buckles.

The minister had been out westerly some miles where a homesteader's wife was dying. He said, 'They ought to make a law about the railroads calling this land they have for sale good for farming. They come out here, kill themselves tryin' to make a living. Well, I didn't mean to mention this but the ride back was long an' I kept thinking. By the way, some hoodlums painted a skeleton with feathers on its head on the spokesman's tombstone night before last.'

Hugh did not speak until he had met the gaze of the eavesdropping liveryman, who hustled towards his harness room with the minister's California light-horse rigging, then he said, 'When I get back I'll help you scrub it off.'

'Will you be gone long, Mister Black?'

'I doubt it, maybe a day or two.'

After they parted and the liveryman, Jim Murphy, parked the rig he went up the back alley to the jailhouse. He visited with the marshal for about half an hour before returning to his barn.

Later, with shadows forming, Arthur Hammond came over from his store. He declined Boyle's offer of coffee, sat down and said, 'He's asked questions around town.'

Boyle nodded, he knew that. He waited for something spectacular and he got it.

Hammond said, 'You got any idea who he is?'

'No sir, I don't,' Boyle replied, as he rocked forward and clasped large hands atop his desk.

'He's kin to that damned In'ian Enoch reburied.'

Boyle continued to lean. Of course! His Horse Is Black and Hugh Black! Boyle gazed at the storekeeper. 'Why is he here, Mister Hammond?'

'I don't know, but you can bet your boots he ain't here for any good.' Hammond arose and moved to the door. 'Marshal, he's goin' to make trouble as sure as you're sittin' there.'

After the storekeeper had departed Marshal Boyle went up to the parsonage where Enoch Severn was diligently scrubbing black paint off an upright tombstone. Enoch arose, flinched from kneeling so long and said, 'I'd like to know who defaced this marker.'

Boyle considered the stone. 'Not much

you could do if you did know, Enoch. Things like this is goin' to happen. If you'd used your head you would have reburied him somewhere a long way off and left off even a headboard.'

They moved to the shade. There were benches in the cemetery, mostly planted where there was shade. As the minister sat down and mopped sweat off he put a quizzical look on the marshal. 'Why do people deface headstones?' he asked, and made a fluttery small gesture with both hands. 'The dead are gone. They have no truck with us. Nothing we do, like painting their headstones, can't mean anythin' to the dead. But it can bother the living.'

Big Marshal Boyle sprawled on his bench. It was beginning to get summer-hot. Spring had not entirely departed but it certainly was being nudged on its way. He said, 'Enoch, tell me what you think of Hugh Black.'

The preacher's gaze remained on the lawman. 'What am I supposed to think? He's a friendly feller. I heard he sewed up Jake Miller's little dog. I only talked with him twice. You want my personal opinion?'

'Somethin' like that.'

'He'd be a credit to the community.'

'Do you know the name of that old bronco you reburied?'

'Certainly. His Horse Is Black.'

'Don't that ring any bells, Enoch?'

'What bells?'

'The stranger's name is Black.'

Severn considered the large man for a moment or two before saying, 'Marshal, there's maybe thousands of people named Black.'

'Yes sir. But not here, an' not someone with that name askin' questions.'

'About what Marshal?'

'Well; that's what's got me stumped. Riders come an' go like autumn leaves. They don't care about the town or folks who live here. This feller asks questions which seem to mean he's interested in our town an' us.'

Preacher Severn looked hard at his guest. He'd heard it said lawmen just naturally read things into events and people because they have suspicious minds and besides that, the coal oil would be drying on the headstone. He stood up. 'Marshal, I don't believe Hugh Black is an outlaw, or whatever you figure he is. I got to get back to work.'

As the lawman walked south in the direction of his jailhouse he was not happy about the ire he'd aroused in the preacher.

After dinner, with the sun directly overhead, he went over to the emporium. It had half a dozen customers, all female with shopping bags. Mister Hammond and his clerk were up to their armpits with customers. He caught Hammond's eye and returned to the jailhouse. Now, he was beginning to doubt that what he was doing about Hugh Black was justified. Maybe he was imagining things, maybe Mister Hammond had been spooked for no reason. It was a widely held opinion that the storekeeper lacked a lot of being lily white, which might have something to do with a thing called conscience. Maybe Mister Hammond had some private reason for worrying about Hugh Black, in which case, providing the law had not been violated, it was his private problem.

Marshal Boyle went over to Clancy's place where there was a poker game in progress some distance from the bar. Clancy reluctantly left the players to meet the lawman across the bar. He said, 'Jim Murphy told me a while back that Hugh Black feller left town early with a bedroll behind his saddle an' grub in his saddle-bags. I figured you'd want to know he's pulled stakes.'

Boyle considered the saloonman in long silence then bobbed his head for beer. By the time Clancy returned with the mug of suds Marshal Boyle had digested the news of Hugh Black leaving town. He saluted Clancy with the glass, drank it half empty, felt better almost immediately and went down the east side of Main Street as far as the bench out front of the emporium and was sitting there when Mister Hammond came up, saw him and sat down.

Boyle said, 'Business is good.'

Hammond nodded, ignored the implication and asked a question. 'Where is he?'

'Hugh Black?'

'Yes. Where is he?'

'Saddled up early an' left town with his bedroll an' saddlebags.' At the look this statement produced in the storekeeper, Marshal Boyle couldn't resist. He said, 'Gone, Mister Hammond. I expect Martindale ain't where he wants to settle after all.'

The storekeeper slumped, watched a top buggy go past which had bright yellow wheels, let go a rough breath and with the lawman watching, Hammond loosened all over. Boyle slapped the other man's leg and shot up to his feet. 'Next time you see a bogey man...''

Hammond watched the large man cross to his jailhouse. He looked both ways in the roadway, arose and went back inside. His relief was great for about an hour, then he fell to brooding. Where had Hugh Black gone? Why had he left? Mister Hammond told the clerk he'd be at his residence and left an apron atop a counter on his way out.

Spring was yielding to summer, most

notably as the days wore on. Nevada was one of those places where at the higher elevations it got colder than a witch's bosom, and in summertime it got hot enough to fry eggs on rocks.

There were forested uplands, there was even a river or two, but taken all in all, Nevada was not an appealing place unless a man was a hard-rock miner or someone employed in services such as freighters, stage drivers, storekeepers and the like, people who made a living there, who relied on an economy which assured a living wage, the kind of situation where, ugly or not, people became dependent on jobs and did not readily leave for more pleasant and attractive places.

It was anyone's guess how long Nevada had been inhabited but within living memory most folks had encountered natives, a slightly less than admirable people called 'Digger Indians' because they relied heavily on things dug from the earth, including grubs, lizards and ants.

In the upland where game was available people called Shoshoni lived at a more advanced stage. They hunted, had more or less permanent places—called rancherias—and were much advanced over the rat-eating, bird-egg-sucking desert Diggers.

Shoshoni had war bonnets, tanned-skin attire, even beadwork. They were more similar to the northward tribesmen, Lakota, Crows, Assiniboin, Dakota and Cheyenne, both northern and southern Cheyenne. In fact miscegenation was not uncommon among the upland Shoshoni and northern tribesmen.

Hugh Black took plenty of time, read landmarks, watched for old tree blazes, found trails worn deep into rock and rode into Abner Holt's meadow by late evening.

He hobbled the horse in knee-high feed, fished in the bisecting creek for his supper, made a little dry-wood fire, bathed all over in the creek and sat on a stone at a place where boulders had been arranged in a cooking circle by people who were no more, until he was dry, then redressed and spread his blankets.

He was comfortable in this still and

broodingly silent place, slept like the dead and awakened in the first streaks of dawn-light to discover he had a visitor, a hungry one who had pawed through everything including his saddle-bags in search for food.

Hugh sat up, said, 'Good morning, *tatanka*,' and was totally ignored.

It was not a young bear. It weighed in the neighbourhood of 500 pounds, had ragged ears and other scars from many fights. It was an animal who had only one enemy—man. Otherwise, other animals left it strictly alone; an enraged bear, or a sow bear with cubs, were the most deadly animals alive.

This bear was interested in food, nothing else. The man sitting up in his bedroll with an ivory-handled six-gun in one fist neither frightened nor interested him. He evidently had not encountered a man before, or, if he had, had not been confronted or shot at.

Hugh yawned, scratched, slid out of his blankets, got dressed and was pulling on his boots when the old boar raised its head and really considered him. Hugh picked up the gun, held it in his lap and spoke quietly. 'You're makin' a mess of my camp, old bones. If you wait a spell I'll catch you some fish.'

The bear neither growled nor pawed dirt.

Hugh went to the creek, caught two fat Dolly Vardens, threw them to the bear and while it was hungrily devouring them, bones and all, Hugh went looking for his horse.

The scent of a bear could inspire a hobbled horse to jump higher and farther than the fastest rabbit on earth. When he found the horse it was wringing wet with sweat and was standing like a rock looking back where the camp was. Hugh left it. He could not have led it or ridden it back, not as long as bear scent was around.

When he returned to the camp the boar bear was gone. He rearranged his camp. Because bears were expert climbers there was no point in hanging his saddlebags or Winchester boot in a tree.

He spent the day fishing, poking around,

found early, obliterated tipi-rounds, fire pits and stone cooking rings.

He also found wolf-worried graves, mostly empty, and two places where large stones has been piled waist-high over graves which scavengers had been unable to dig through.

He sat on a large tan rock listening to the creek. Sat there almost two hours before catching fish for two meals and returning to camp to lie back with pine-scented stillness all around. When he made a little cooking fire inside one of the ancient rings of stones for his supper he got a feeling of being watched and slowly twisted to look around.

The old boar was back but this time he sat on his haunches watching the two-legged creature with its fire. The bear was over there until dusk arrived, then got up on all fours, turned and disappeared among trees and gathering shadows.

Hugh Black never saw the bear again.

In the morning he brought the horse back and while it stood nervous and wary, he rigged it out, tied the bedroll into place, buckled the saddle boot with the Winchester butt-plate backwards beneath the *rosadero*, called to the bear and started back the way he had come.

It was a long ride. Once he got clear of the uplands and their pungent-scented pines and firs, he encountered heat. By late afternoon it was hot enough for heat-waves to make distant objects seem to be floating, undulating, swaying in an atmosphere which was smoke-like in its ability to blur distances.

By the time he had Martindale's rooftops in sight, while the heat hadn't lessened, the sun was little more than a curved rash descending beyond some obscure but very real high rims.

He rode down the west-side alley and entered the livery barn from out back.

The liveryman had left earlier. His nighthawk was sitting on a bench near the harness room and watched a man leading a horse come up the runway.

The night hostler went to help with the off-saddling. Black was looping the latigo, preparing to shift the saddle to his shoulder and told the nightman to hold the harness-room door open for him.

The last thing he did before heading for the eatery was watch the nighthawk spill a coffee tin full of rolled barley in the feed box for his horse, and watch the hostler scamper up the loft ladder to pitch down sweet-smelling timothy hay.

When he entered the café several diners looked up. They looked startled and they were. Talk had spread through town earlier that the dark-eyed stranger had left the country.

# 5

## Cranky Jake Miller

Arnold Boyle swore a blue streak when Andy Sears, the town blacksmith, told him the big, cross-tied breedy-looking horse belonged to Hugh Black. Andy wasn't shocked at the language but he was impressed by its vehemence. Marshal Boyle's temper was notorious, but why he exploded over seeing Hugh Black's horse ready to be fitted with a new set of shoes was beyond him. He approached the horse, ran a gentling hand down its neck and talked to it. If it was the big bay that had set the marshal off, then it behoved Sears to be wary.

When the marshal entered the emporium the clerk was caring for a tall, rawboned woman with a mouth like a bear trap. She and the clerk watched as Boyle stamped through the store, flung open the door of Mister Hammond's cubbyhole office and slammed it closed after himself. The clerk cleared his throat and the woman went back to reading from her grocery list as though nothing had happened. It so happened that what was required to upset her was something more than an angry lawman stamping through a store.

Arthur Hammond was doing his ledgers. Under normal circumstances he did not welcome intrusions. For all his success as a businessman he loathed bookkeeping, ciphers of any kind, and the prospect of bringing the ledgers current was something he invariably put off until the last minute.

He turned to snarl at the interruption but did not have the opportunity. Marshal Boyle glared as he said, 'Black didn't leave the country! His horse is bein' shod down yonder. Mister Hammond, right from the start I've had a feelin' you got an idea why he's here, and I want to know what it is, *right damned now!*'

The last three words carried into the store and while the clerk flinched his rawboned customer did not interrupt her litany of articles she wanted.

Mister Hammond rocked back in his chair. He knew the lawman's temperament as well as other folks did. Also, while it had been years since anyone had approached him as Boyle had, right now that did not matter. He was looking at a very large, very angry man.

He managed to say, 'What's got into you? You know as much about that son of a bitch as I do.'

'Mister Hammond, I think you're a liar!'

Again the portly merchant was taken aback. 'I told you he's not here for any good.'

'I know you told me that. Now I want to know why he ain't.'

Arthur Hammond fished for a handkerchief and mopped his forehead, put the handkerchief away and stared at the large man standing less than ten feet from where he was sitting. He said, 'Sit down, Marshal.'

Boyle did not move.

Hammond's gaze slid away and did not return to the lawman's face. 'I think Hugh Black is kin to His Horse Is Black.'

The marshal growled about that. It didn't take much sense to figure that out. 'Go on!'

'Well; years back, long before you come here, long before we had a bank, before...'

'Get to the gawddamned point, Mister Hammond!'

'More'n twenty years ago that In'ian come to town with a paper he showed to fellers who were on the council back then—only two or three of us left now.'

'What about the paper!'

'It was an old treaty between the gov'ment an' the Shoshoni.'

Marshal Boyle went to a chair, sat down and leaned forward looking at the storekeeper. 'What did the paper say?' he asked.

Again, Mister Hammond fished out the handkerchief and mopped his face and neck. 'It give some land to the Shoshoni in perpetuity.'

'In what?'

'Perpetuity. It means forever.'

Marshal Boyle leaned back, shoved out his feet and seemed to relax. 'Tell me if I'm wrong,' he told the storekeeper. 'The piece of paper give the Shoshoni all their land by treaty.'

'That's right, Marshal.'

'An' tell me if I'm wrong this time. Martindale is settin' on land that was given 'em by treaty?'

'But they're gone, Marshal. There's no Shoshoni left. The army took 'em away.'

Marshal Boyle made a noisy sigh. 'An' that means folks can take the land given In'ians in a treaty?'

'Somethin' like that,' Hammond said, then became less hesitant and defensive. 'The law says abandoned property, like that old hotel at the lower end of town, becomes the property of them as make use of it when there's no one left to dispute claim of ownership. You understand?'

'Why didn't you tell me this before?'

'I figured you knew. Most folks do.'

'Your store's on treaty land?'

'Yes, but so is Clancy's place, so is

85

other stores, even your jailhouse is on treaty land. Marshal, do you expect we're goin' to give everythin' back to a bunch of heathen that we don't even know where they are?'

Boyle sat motionless, hands across his middle, gazing at Arthur Hammond. 'Tell me somethin'? Is that why you're afraid of Hugh Black? Because you figure he's a Shoshoni come back to make folks mind the treaty?'

Hammond avoided a direct reply. He said, 'Marshal, think about it. If the In'ians own where the jailhouse stands, you got no job. If they own where the saloon is, Clancy's out of business. If they own where my store'n house stands, I'm not only out of business, I got no place to live.'

For a long moment big Arnold Boyle sat like a buddha, silent and expressionless, then he gripped the arms of his chair and shoved up to his feet. 'What you just said, Mister Hammond, is that one Shoshoni can ride in here and maybe get the army to back up some damned old treaty made twenty–thirty years ago.'

The storekeeper fished out his handkerchief for the third time and while mopping sweat he said, 'That's the long and short of it, Marshal. Now you know why that son or grandson of old His Horse Is Black set me to worryin' until I can't sleep. One damned In'ian can ruin Martindale and most of the folks in it.' Hammond held the handkerchief away from his face looking squarely at Marshal Boyle. 'Unless he had an accident. A fatal accident.'

The lawman left Hammond's store, hiked over to his jailhouse, sat down and groped for his secret bottle. When he stowed it back in the box beneath his desk he said, 'Son of a bitch!'

He sat there for a good half hour staring at the far wall. The more he thought the more he wondered. If Mister Hammond was right.... What he had to do was find out all he could about Hugh Black, who did not fit the description of most Indians he had seen and, as he surmised, the name Black did not have to mean Hugh Black was kin to an Indian someone had murdered twenty years earlier, but it sure as hell could.

He abruptly sat straight up in his chair. It was now common knowledge His Horse Is Black had his skull crushed by someone behind him, which was murder any way folks looked at it. What made him sit up was a fresh and unpleasant thought: had Arthur Hammond killed the Indian? If not, would Hammond know who did?

Marshal Boyle's temperament seemed to change over the following days. Folks assumed he was surly when in fact it was not that at all. He waylaid Arthur Hammond at Clancy's place one night. They discussed many things but said nothing about their conversation in the storekeeper's office, but Marshal Boyle left the saloon early and was waiting outside in the darkness when Hammond emerged.

The marshal, always direct, incapable of guile, put the question to the storekeeper out front of the saloon with no one around.

'Did you kill His Horse Is Black?'

As at other times, Boyle's directness

shocked Arthur Hammond. He replied in an unsteady voice which would not have convinced many people he was telling the truth, but startling people could have an identical effect. He said, 'No!'

Marshal Boyle considered the portly man over a moment of silence before speaking again. 'But you know who did.'

'Marshal, for Chris' sake that was more'n twenty years ago. You'd do well to leave it lie, everyone else does.' Hammond brushed past, indignation making him walk as though he had a ramrod up his back.

The following morning Marshal Boyle employed the same waylaying tactic in front of the hotel. When Hugh Black emerged the lawman was waiting. He asked Black to accompany him to the jailhouse and although Hugh hadn't had breakfast he walked beside the larger man, sat down and gave Boyle look for look until the lawman said, 'It's none of my affair, but I was wonderin' where you went yestiddy.'

Hugh answered easily. 'For a long

horseback ride. Toward the hills an' around.'

Boyle almost sounded sarcastic when he said, 'Feller'd like to get to know country he might figure settlin' in. Right?'

Hugh smiled. 'It'd be a good thing to do. No harm in it is there?'

As he'd done other times with Hugh Black, Marshal Boyle would not be distracted by questions. He leaned on the desk. 'You was born in the Territory?'

'I told you I was.'

'In'ian Territory, Mister Black. That makes you an In'ian, wouldn't it?'

Hugh used Boyle's tactic against him. He did not answer the question, instead he asked one of his own. 'Did you know all this country used to belong to In'ians?'

Marshal Boyle eased back slowly off his desk. So Hammond had been right. Black had a reason for being here which had nothing to do with settling in.

The dark-eyed man spoke again. 'In'ian Territory was given to tribesmen from all over. It was their country. Then you know what happened? The government opened it to settlers, had 'em line up for miles, fired a gun an' they over-run everything, the sacred ground given In'ians for their homeland forever included.'

Marshal Boyle had encountered his share of bitter Indians. This one didn't sound bitter even when he spoke about the Oklahoma rush. In fact he smiled when he said, 'Whites didn't treat their own kind any better, but In'ians didn't either. I guess a man could say treaties, promises or skin colour don't matter when it comes to somethin' like free land.'

Marshal Boyle recognized the opportunity Hugh Black had just given him but lacked the ability to put it into words and the mention of land and land-rights did not occur again during their visit, but after Hugh Black had left the lawman was willing to believe Arthur Hammond's notion concerning the reason why Hugh Black was in Martindale. It had to do with land, the land Indians had been deprived of by force.

He leaned back, both hands clasped behind his head. Twenty years was a long time, damned near a lifetime, and what could one Indian—he sure as hell wasn't a full-blood—what could a 'breed Indian do against an entire community that had the law on its side? Not a damned thing, and if he made trouble the marshal would take care of that. He had taken an oath to uphold the law.

That evening just short of dusk, Jim Murphy, the liveryman, brought him a new headache. Four Indians had appeared at the lower end of town, one full-blood and three 'breeds. They had made a camp near to the creek that supplied town water and ran free where it exited Martindale to the south.

Boyle scowled. 'How do you know that?' he asked Murphy.

'My night man was returning from deliverin' light freight for the store an' seen 'em. He said he waved an' they waved back.'

'It could have been someone else. Travellers passin' through.'

Murphy slowly and emphatically shook

his head. 'It was In'ians.' My nighthawk grew up among 'em.'

After the liveryman left Marshal Boyle went to the café looking for Hugh Black, who was not there. He visited Clancy's saloon, the rooming-house, even the harness works. No one had seen Hugh Black.

It was getting along, shadows were forming on the east side of buildings when he went out back, saddled and bridled a horse and kept to the alley until he was beyond town, then angled as far as the roadway and while riding southward kept watching the easterly area where the creek ran.

It had thickets of willows, it also had cottonwood tress and areas of flourishing undergrowth. He saw no hobbled animal and no Indians, no supper fire, not even any sign, but dusk was approaching. He rode almost two miles before turning back.

This time he rode over to the creek where grass grew fifty or seventy-five feet from the watercourse. He dismounted and led his animal,

He found barefoot horse sign, found where animals had chewed on willows, had left droppings in the tall grass and finally, where men had been.

It got too dark to track the strangers beyond soft earth so he mounted and rode back toward town.

By the time he got to the café most of the customary diners had eaten and departed, which was just as well because Arnold Boyle was not in a good mood.

Where had the four Indians gone? Who were they? And it troubled him that four more tomahawks were in his bailiwick who probably knew Hugh Black.

He did not sleep well that night. He would not have slept at all if he had known where Hugh Black was; part way toward that old rancheria, and he was not alone.

In the morning he caught the proprietor early to ascertain whether Black was still in his room, and should have anticipated the reply he got.

'How would I know? I rent rooms. Spyin' on folks who stay here ain't in the agreement about busted winders, fights and comin' in drunk an' noisy. Go bang on the door.'

Marshal Boyle returned to the hallway and knocked, about half convinced Black would not be inside, but he was, and opened the door fully clothed, hair slicked and shaven. He greeted the dour-faced large man pleasantly. 'Come in, Marshal.'

Boyle stepped past the door, his eyes searching every nook and cranny as Hugh Black closed the door, moved around front and said, 'What can I do for you, Marshal?'

Boyle scowled. 'You can tell me about them four friends of your'n.'

'What four friends?'

'Four In'ians that tanked up their horses alongside Willow Creek east of town.'

'Friends of mine, Marshal?'

Boyle had a quicksand feeling where he stood. He began to waver. 'There's been no In'ians around Martindale since before I come here,' he said.

'But there were before you came in, Marshal, an' there are In'ians pretty much

95

everywhere. This was their country, they still wander around in it. Is there a law says they can't do that?'

Boyle reddened. He had exchanged words with Hugh Black before. He began to feel foolish. 'You don't know four tomahawks that just showed up?'

'Showed up when?'

'Well, maybe yestiddy, I ain't sure exactly when they showed up. I better tell you, friend, folks are beginnin' to wonder about you, me among 'em.'

When he said this Marshal Boyle reached behind himself for the door latch. He continued to show a menacing look as he opened the door, stepped through and slammed the door.

All the way to his jailhouse the back of his neck was red. He was inserting the large brass key into the padlock when the liveryman came scuttling over from the café. He said, 'You find 'em?'

'Find who?' the lawman growled as he pocketed the lock and pushed the door open.

'Them four warwhoops. I see you ride

south from the alley last evenin'. Did you find 'em?'

Boyle said, 'No!' and slammed the roadway door. Jim Murphy, acquainted with the large man's irascibility, shrugged and hiked southward to his livery barn.

Jake Miller entered the jailhouse looking like he'd been sucking lemons, his normal expression, and said, 'Well, you smelled any flowers lately, Marshal?'

Boyle, who was not in the mood for this stood behind his desk glaring. 'You got somethin' to say, Jake, spit it out or get the hell out of here. I got work to do.'

Miller was unfazed, he had weathered the large man's moods many times. 'Yeah, smellin' springtime flowers. My safe was busted open last night and cleaned out down to the last red cent, an' there was six gold bars in it an' two thousand dollars to be taken south this mornin'.'

Marshal Boyle stood like a statue. Jake Miller made a sneering smile. 'If you can spare the time from flower-sniffin' I'd take it kindly if you'd run down them sons of bitches, get the money an' bars back an' hang 'em on the spot. Plenty of time, Mister Boyle, they only been on the run since about one in the morning, six, seven hours ago. But you'n the eleven-hundred pound, pudding-footed horse of yours can run 'em down.' Miller went to the door, turned and said, 'If he can sprout wings.'

News of the robbery spread; in a place like Martindale things like robbery, gossip, wild tales spread like wildfire. By the time Marshal Boyle appeared at the corralyard office to look at the safe, what had happened was beginning to spread even beyond town.

Jake Miller hopped around Boyle like an aged cricket pointing out that the safe had not been dynamited, had not been forced with crowbars, but there it was, wide open with papers scattered, two lightly oiled rags on the floor which had previously held gold bars, and several empty little buckskin pouches with puckered draw strings which were empty. Miller said they had been full like the other sacks of the same kind which were missing.

The corralyard whose three hostlers were

usually busy mornings mingled with what seemed to be half the population of Martindale when the lawman left heading for the corral behind the jailhouse.

He made a wide sashay around the town, tried to single out four unshod horse tracks from dozens of other tracks and did not succeed until he widened his search to the point where tracks were fewer and mostly made by shod animals. He picked up the sign of four barefoot horses going northward.

He was convinced in his heart those four mysterious Indians were responsible for the robbery. He had no particular reason to believe this beyond a hunch, but right at that moment no one could have convinced him otherwise.

# 6

## Facts and Answers

He didn't see the stationary horseman who was backgrounded by the brushy, timbered hills until his saddle animal threw up its head. It hadn't seen the man either but it had caught the scent of his horse.

Marshal Boyle straightened in the saddle, up to this point tracking hadn't been difficult. It did not occur to him at the time that the tracks he had been following were too clear, too obvious, to have been made by fugitive Indians, masters of every ancient method of disguising sign.

He wasn't even thinking of Indians when his horse threw up its head, he had been thinking of outlaws, the kind that robbed safes, experienced, seasoned thieves. He had never heard of Indians breaking into steel safes.

He approached the distant rider without haste. In turn, the horseman sat like a statue. When they were close enough Marshal Boyle said, 'You!'

The other rider smiled. 'You read sign pretty well, Marshal.'

Boyle snorted. 'It was plain as day. Was that the idea, Mister Black?'

That made the other man laugh but he did not reply to the question. 'Whose tracks are you dogging, Marshal?'

Boyle evened-up his reins without answering nor looking up. When he rested both hands atop the saddle horn he put an unwavering gaze upon Hugh Black. 'Did you ever hear of In'ians robbing a safe, Mister Black?'

'In town?'

'The stage company's safe. Sometime last night?'

'In'ians?'

'Well, the tracks led up here. Four riders. There was four broncos camped south of town yestiddy.'

101

'So, they robbed the safe?'

Boyle had developed an aversion to arguing with Hugh Black. He looped both reins, dismounted and loosened the cinch before facing the mounted man. 'You tell me. Did they rob the safe?'

'I wasn't there, Marshal. I can't say.'

Boyle put a sardonic gaze on the mounted man. 'Someday,' he said dryly, 'I'm goin' to get a direct answer out of you.'

Again Hugh Black smiled. He did not dismount but he leaned on his saddle swells. 'Follow the sign, Marshal. You got any idea where it'll take you?'

'Maybe.'

'Where?'

'A few miles on up through there's a big meadow. In'ians had a rancheria there until the army rounded 'em up and took them away.'

'You know the place, Marshal?'

'Well, I've been up there huntin', but that was some years ago.'

Hugh Black raised his left hand with the reins in it. 'Follow me,' he said, and did not look back to ascertain whether the lawman was a-horseback behind him. He was.

There was no conversation until they reached a busy little freshwater creek tumbling among rocks. There, Hugh Black swung off, slipped the bridle and leaned on his saddle as the horse drank. Marshal Boyle did the same.

When Hugh was rebridling he said, 'You known Arthur Hammond long?'

Boyle answered matter-of-factly as he also rebridled. 'Ever since I come here.'

'And Murphy, the liveryman; Sears, the blacksmith?'

'Yes, they were here too.'

Hugh snugged the cinch, and stepped over leather before speaking again. 'An' the cranky old bastard who runs the stage company?'

'Jake Miller? I know him as well as I want to. Why?'

'One more, Marshal. The saloonman?'

'Clancy Harney. What are you gettin' at?'

Hugh did not answer nor look around

as they began a gradual climb, working their way back and forth among forest giants that were in places too close for riders to stay abreast. When they reached the top-out Hugh halted, let his reins sag and gazed down into a huge park of grass with occasional stands of buck-brush.

There was a fire down there. Its smoke rose straight up in a lazy spiral. There were horses grazing. Hugh pointed. 'That's where the tracks would have led you.'

Marshal Boyle squinted. He could make out men where the smoke was rising but was unable to count them except that there were more than four of them.

Hugh angled westerly as far as an ancient trail which, in places, was worn through rock. He kicked both feet clear of the stirrups, a practice common among horsemen riding a steep downhill trail that had patches of rock.

Marshal Boyle did the same. He watched for the patches of slick rock. His horse was shod, which under the circumstances was an invitation to disaster unless the rider was very careful, which the marshal was.

When they reached grass country the sidehill with its stands of huge old over-ripe firs and pines backgrounded them. Boyle eased his feet into the stirrups, let the reins sway loose and because his horse followed Hugh Black's horse, the lawman could concentrate on that distant smoke.

When they were closer the marshal said, 'Friends of yours?'

Hugh offered a delayed reply. 'Some of them.'

The men at the fire watched the horsemen approach. Two unwound up off the ground, wiped their hands on their trousers and stood like statues. The other men at the cooking fire remained on the ground.

Marshal Boyle let go a soundless long sigh. Each of the townsmen Black had asked about were among the seated men.

Where they dismounted the pair of standing men came over to take care of their animals. Hugh led the lawman to the fire where Boyle eyed the townsmen. He also considered two Indians seated with them. The Indians were armed, none of

105

the townsmen was.

Hugh pointed to a spit made of green limbs where a deer haunch was cooking. 'No coffee,' he said. 'Help yourself to breakfast, Marshal.'

Boyle ignored the fire ring and its tantalizing aroma. He addressed the portly man nearest him. 'Mister Hammond?'

The storekeeper looked up without saying a word.

Boyle spoke to Clancy, who was never without words, except this time. He looked up at Marshal Boyle while wiping his hands on a greasy bandana, all without saying a word.

Hugh Black gestured for the lawman to squat, which Boyle did. The men who had hobbled the horses out in tall grass returned, sat down without looking at Hugh or the marshal, and with razor-sharp fleshing knives carved pieces of well-cooked meat off the haunch. They were Indians, stalwart, muscular men with black hair and eyes, several with fairer colouring than full-bloods had. Their behaviour was pure Indian. They ignored everything but the meat they were eating.

Arthur Hammond wiped his lower face and seemed about to speak. A fleshing knife swerved close to his throat. Hammond instinctively sucked back. The knife went to the cooking meat where it was used to make a slice and the portly storekeeper looked helplessly at Marshal Boyle.

Hugh sliced a piece of meat, held it on the tip of his knife toward the marshal, who took the meat and began eating.

He knew what this was about. He had never sat through an Indian palaver himself but he had heard about them, how they were conducted. His father and uncle had sat through them. As a youngster their stories had made his hair stand up. Even if their stories hadn't done that, his position here would have instinctively urged caution. Four unarmed townsmen and himself could not buck the kind of odds that put men in cemeteries from Montana to Mexico and from the Big Muddy to New Mexico Territory. For all his fierce temper, Arnold Boyle was not in a situation where he would be entirely surprised or angered.

Hugh Black sat cross-legged and ate for a while, wiped his hands and gazed at the town marshal with no trace of rancour as he spoke. 'These men knew about the killing of His Horse Is Black.' Hugh paused. 'His Horse Is Black was my grandfather. I wanted you with us when we made judgment.'

The one incorrigible among the townsmen who could have been relied upon not to obey the injunction against any of the townsmen speaking until spoken to, railed at Marshal Boyle.

'Smellin' flowers, was you? I've told the council for years they'd ought to give the badge to a younger man. Look at what happened last night, an' you knowin' nothin' until that 'breed led you in here. Fine lawman you—'

The Indian's backhanded blow nearly toppled Jake backwards. It would have, considering his bird-like build, if the blow had been hard. It was intended to quiet the stager. At least for a while it accomplished that.

Boyle flung meat scraps into the fire ring, hitched up one cheek to reach his handkerchief and made a very thorough job of wiping his hands and face. He then caught Hugh Black's gaze and held it. 'I'm waitin',' he said.

Black wiped his hands on grass, ran a sleeve across his lower face and returned the lawman's unwavering gaze as he said, 'Do you know who killed His Horse Is Black?'

Boyle shook his head.

'We do. Did you know a man named Corey Kincade?'

Again the lawman shook his head.

Old Jake couldn't resist. 'I told you. Boyle didn't come to the Martindale country for about five, six years after—'

This time the Indian's blow was more than a backhand. Old Jake went violently sideward. There was a trickle of blood from his mouth.

Hugh Black spoke as though there had been no interruption. 'We know who hired Kincade to kill His Horse Is Black. We know how much Kincade was paid for the killing.' Hugh finished wiping his hands, tucked the cloth away and looked steadily at the lawman.

Boyle was scowling. 'These gents did that?'

'Two arranged for it, Marshal. The others chipped in the money.'

'Where is Kincade?'

This time Hugh nodded in the direction of Clancy Harney. 'Tell him.'

'He's in the graveyard. Someone shot him in the back a few months after the old In'ian was killed. We never knew who shot him, but it wasn't much of a loss.'

Old Jake was sitting up holding a bandana to his split lip. If he was in pain, what was transpiring made him ignore discomfort. He was about to speak again when the bronco on his left raised his knife to Jake's gullet and held it there. Hugh spoke to the Indian. 'Let him talk.' When the knife was removed Jake used the first moment to glare murderously at the Indian before speaking.

'All right. You snuck us up here early this morning. We been palaverin' since then and nothing's been settled.' Jake put his bitter stare on the storekeeper. 'Get it over with, Hammond.'

The portly man did not say a word, he sat looking steadily at the stager. Murphy, the liveryman, picked up a twig and concentrated on making scratches on the ground. He was ignored. Clancy Harney meticulously rolled a smoke. None of them looked at either the storekeeper or the stager, but when Clancy was trickling smoke, cranky Jake Miller spoke again. He looked at Hugh Black when he said, 'They won't tell you. Not the truth anyway. You know who killed the old man an' now you know that son of a bitch is buried.' Jake paused to spear Arthur Hammond with another bitter stare. 'Tell them, 'possum belly. If you don't I will.'

Marshal Boyle ignored the storekeeper. 'Spit it out,' he told Jake Miller.

Jake did. 'The spokesman come to the town council with his treaty paper. It warn't a surprise. Most of us settin' here remember when the army brought some fellers from Washington to palaver with the

In'ians. When the old tomahawk come to town with his paper he laid it on the line. We knew about the treaty but went ahead an' built Martindale anyway.

'His Horse Is Black told the council we was on In'ian land. The treaty said so. He said they'd go to the gov'ment an' the army for what we done.

'After he left, the council figured to let things slide for a spell.' Jake nodded toward Arthur Hammond before concluding what he had to say. 'That's what you said, Arthur, let things slide. You said troubles had a way of settlin' themselves.' Jake paused one more time. When he spoke again his voice dripped sarcasm. 'The council done nothin' because His Horse Is Black never got back to the rancheria. He just upped and disappeared. That was the same night he come before the council. Hammond, you got anythin' to say? How about you, Clancy? Andy? Jim, you want to put in two-bits' worth?'

None of them spoke but Marshal Boyle did. 'So there was a conspiracy an' the In'ian was killed by a feller named Kincade, who is now dead an' buried. You can't turn back the clock. What's done is done.' He looked up at Hugh Black who was standing with arms crossed looking steadily at Jake Miller. 'You want to scalp 'em, Mister Black? The law'll hunt you down like a rat forever how long it takes.'

The other Indians sat like stones. One of them looked at the storekeeper. 'Tell your part,' he said.

Hammond squirmed, looked at the lawman, at Clancy, Jim Murphy, Sears, and lastly at the stager.

'For a fact it was long ago. Every man settin' here was buildin' up a business. Everythin' we had was in what we was doin', makin' Martindale a busy town. We brought in the bank an' the telegraph.'

Hugh said, 'So you took up a collection and had His Horse Is Black killed.'

Hammond fished forth a large cloth and mopped off sweat. 'What was the Shoshoni goin' to do with the land? Nothing. They'd owned it for hunnerts of years an' never ploughed a furrow, opened a store, built a decent house.'

'What about their treaty rights?' Hugh asked.

Hammond squirmed. 'Someday we'd have gone to them with money for the land.'

Hugh snorted. 'Why didn't you do that first?'

Jake Miller spoke bluntly. 'Because the Shoshoni wouldn't have sold, an' you know that for a fact. This was huntin' an' campin' country to them. They wouldn't never have done nothin' with it.'

'They didn't have to,' Hugh Black stated. 'It was their land, to live on as they liked, as they always had lived. But you killed His Horse Is Black before you made an offer. I don't think you ever would have made an offer, not after the army came and took the people away. I don't believe you'd ever have done a damned thing if I hadn't come along.'

Marshal Boyle arose and stretched. The sun was climbing. He faced Hugh Black. 'Now tell me you fellers didn't raid the safe at Miller's office.'

Hugh made his slow smile. 'For part

payment, Marshal. We figure what we got pays for the land the corralyard stands on.'

Now, the liveryman, storekeeper, saloon owner and blacksmith looked straight at Hugh Black without one of them making a sound. It had dawned on them why they had been abducted from town and brought to this place. Robbing Jake Miller's safe had been done deliberately to satisfy the Shoshoni, and to put their plan of redemption in motion.

Arthur Hammond spoke to Hugh Black. 'All right. We should've done different, but in them days men thought an' acted different.'

Hugh nodded. 'Kill a troublesome tomahawk. But that was twenty year ago. If you want to figure things accordin' to those days we'd be justified in hangin' every man jack of you.'

Marshal Boyle prepared to speak but Hugh Black cut him off with a sharp gesture. He did not take his eyes off the storekeeper. He had a little more to say before he would allow an interruption and he said it with the sun standing high.

'Our spokesman was killed. We came here to find the man who killed him, an' we found him—buried. So we had one more thing to do. You pay the Shoshoni for the land you stole.' Hugh Black paused. 'Or we hang you here in the rancheria.'

Again Marshal Boyle would have spoken but this time it was Arthur Hammond who said, 'How much?'

'Two thousand dollars from each of you.'

Clancy's eyes sprang wide. Jim Murphy dropped his twig. Andy Sears started up. Jake Miller gasped. Arthur Hammond alone did not look stunned. 'All right. Come by the store.'

Hugh slowly shook his head. 'No. You bring the money up here. Each one of you. Two thousand dollars in greenbacks.'

Hugh finally faced the lawman. 'Take 'em back with you, Marshal, you're a witness to what they agreed to. One more thing, Marshal, we cut the telegraph line last night. Just see that they get the money an' come back up here, by themselves or

116

with you. Marshal, no army, no posse, just them an' you.'

The Indians brought in horses, silently and impassively rigged them for riding and handed out reins. Marshal Boyle's large animal was as full as a tick and looked it. The marshal was standing on the left side to mount when he turned to address Hugh Black.

'They'll have the right to legal title for their land.'

Hugh smiled. 'We drew up a treaty. I got it in my saddle-bags.'

'Well, maybe the law'd want somethin' better, legal an' all.'

'The treaty is legal, Marshal. It was pretty much copied from the other treaty.'

Boyle rose up over leather and while evening his lines and looking down at the Indians, he shook his head.

Hugh Black said, 'This treaty is forever. We don't go back on our word an' we don't steal land just because we know white-man law'll back us up.'

Marshal Boyle led off toward the distant tree-covered uplands. Not a word was said until the riders reached the top-out and hesitated to look back, then, Jake Miller said, 'I'll kill that son of a bitch that hit me.'

They started down the southerly slope in the direction of Martindale with Boyle up front as silent as a stone while he reviewed the entire situation in his mind.

Hugh Black had deliberately left readable sign. He had been waiting for the marshal.

Boyle swore to himself. The biggest mistake whites had made was to set up schools on reservations. He grudgingly conceded that Hugh Black was one *coyote* bronco, and that was another mistake folks had made: tipi Indians of twenty years ago couldn't read or write, were so backward in comparison to their grandchildren it was difficult to believe they came from the same stock.

That easy-going son of a bitch with the ivory-stocked belt-gun must have perfected his plan over many months.

As for the $2000 dollars each of the townsmen had to give the Indians, hell, most men even in cities didn't make $2000 in a year.

The solemn, silent horsemen behind the marshal would almost prefer to shed blood rather than part with that kind of money. There was an excellent chance the liveryman wouldn't have that much. There was an equally excellent chance that Jake Miller would only pay if his life depended on it.

# 7

## A Time of Crisis

They met the second night after their return to town in Clancy's card room with the drape closed. Clancy's stand-in bartender took care of customers, several of whom were intrigued by six of Martindale's prominent citizens meeting in the card room with the drape closed. The substitute barman could tell them nothing. He hadn't even known there was to be a palaver.

It was a warm night, the kind that required anxious men to call for beer, which the barman brought. Arthur Hammond passed cigars around. Jake shook his head, so did Marshal Boyle, but the blacksmith, Andy Sears, lit up from the match Jim Murphy held for Arthur Hammond.

Hammond leaned back from the table.

His paunch discouraged leaning on it. He said, 'Well, gents. Do we have the money?'

Jim Murphy shook his head. 'I scraped up half but I got to sell some livestock and whatnot to get all of it, an' that'll take time.'

Hammond nodded. 'They didn't say when we was to bring 'em the money.'

Marshal Boyle emptied his beer glass and set it down hard. He frowned at the storekeeper whom he thought would have little trouble digging up $2000. 'My feelin' is that they won't wait more'n a few days.'

Jim Murphy threw up his hands. 'I plain out can't get it that fast. Not even if I knock down my usin' animals by the pound.'

Clancy leaned off the table. He had the $2000 and would have bet his life so did the storekeeper. He looked at Sears, who was holding his cigar out looking pleased. When he saw the saloonman and the others watching him, he said, 'I about got it. Take another day or two.' He plugged the cigar back into his mouth. 'They sure as hell don't expect all of us to come up with that kind of money overnight. We ain't like In'ians; we don't live off the gov'ment. We got to sweat for our money.'

That statement by the blacksmith set old Jake off. He abruptly pushed his half-empty beer glass aside and leaned forward. 'I'm agin' it. I'm agin givin' them tomahawks one red cent. What they done was break the law capturin' us out of our beds an' takin' us up there, scairin' the whey out of us then tryin' pure an' simple blackmail. I tell you gents you can count me out. I been...'

Hammond interrupted to say, 'Jake, I don't agree with 'em no more'n you do. Less, I expect. But we're settin' on a keg of dynamite.'

'Is that a fact? What can they do? We can call in the army.'

Hammond interrupted again. 'I'll tell you what they can do. As for settin' up there until we can get soldiers, Jake, that'd take weeks an' you know it.'

'All right; tell me what five damned In'ians can do?'

Hammond looked straight at the stager when he replied. 'Set the town afire. Five of 'em could do that any night.'

There was an abrupt, long silence during which the blacksmith snuffed out his cigar, made sure there was no fire left and carefully pocketed the stub.

Hammond's remark even took the wind out of Jake Miller's sail, his corralyard and office were made of slab-wood and bone-dry fir poles. None of them said anything, each man thought of his property, every structure in Martindale was wood, either slab-wood or logs; fires started in different places would burn the town to the ground, bucket brigades notwithstanding.

The bartender poked his head past the drapery with cocked eyebrows, Clancy scowled and shook his head. The bartender departed and returned with a pitcher of beer.

Andy Sears made a weak comment. 'We could roust out the possemen, have 'em stand guard all night.'

Jake scotched that idea in a snarl. 'You don't know much about tomahawks or you wouldn't say something like that. Them devils can slip into a town surrounded by soldiers, fire the place and run off all the livestock without no one knowin' until they smelt smoke.'

Arthur Hammond sat through this gloomy moment, hands clasped across his stomach, squinting at the distant drapery. When Marshal Boyle addressed him Hammond pulled himself back from wherever his thoughts had been with an effort, and said, 'One thing might help.' He looked at the liveryman. 'I'll loan you whatever you can't rake up. You too, Andy.'

Again silence settled. The liveryman and blacksmith exchanged a look and did not speak until Marshal Boyle said, 'That's fair, gents,' and Mister Hammond smiled benevolently.

Andrew Sears sounded annoyed when he spoke next. 'I'll carry my own load, Mister Hammond.'

The storekeeper nodded and looked at

Murphy. The liveryman cleared his throat before speaking. 'How much interest, Mister Hammond?'

The storekeeper made a generous gesture and smiled. 'Whatever the bank's chargin', Jim.'

'You gents are overlookin' somethin'. Most of what them savages stole from my safe is more'n any one of 'em makes in a year an' that's enough. Denver won't like that much, let alone givin' them bastards any more.'

Marshal Boyle rolled his eyes. 'Jake, you ain't been listenin'. Even if we got federal marshals they couldn't get here in less than ten days an' them tomahawks aren't goin' to wait more'n another day or two.'

The stager glared. 'Won't make no difference. The army'll come, run them In'ians down an' take 'em back to its prisoner compound.'

Andy Sears spoke sarcastically to the stager. 'An' we'll stand ankle deep in ashes watchin' them go. Jake, there's times when I don't believe you hear real good.'

Before Miller could explode the marshal

spoke curtly. 'I'd guess they'll set there no longer'n day after tomorrow. We got to have the money before then.' He held up a hand toward old Jake to avoid an interruption, lowered the hand and finished what he had to say. 'We got all day tomorrow to raise the money. Andy?'

'I'll have it by afternoon tomorrow.'

'Mister Hammond?'

The storekeeper did not speak, he simply nodded.

'Jim?'

The liveryman spread his hands. 'Not by tomorrow. Not by two weeks from tomorrow.'

Hammond fixed the liveryman with an unwavering look. 'How much'll you need?' he asked.

Murphy leaned on the table with loosely clasped hands. 'The full amount.'

Hammond did not bat an eye. 'Come by the store in the mornin'. I'll have a promissory note for you to sign an' give you the money.'

Clancy was leaning back, both hands plunged deep into trouser pockets. He did not look at any of them when he said, 'I'll have it ready tomorrow.' He raised his eyes to the lawman. 'You goin' to take it up there to 'em?'

Boyle replied curtly. 'Alone. There'd be no way for more'n one of us to get up there without them watchin' us all the way.'

'That's a heap of money, Marshal. More'n most men make in ten years.'

Arnold Boyle gazed at the saloonman. He thought he might have detected a tone of voice he hadn't liked. 'I'll take you along, if you want to go. But only you.'

Clancy replied dryly. 'I got a business to run,' and the marshall smiled without humour. 'Sure you have. You all have.' He stood up. 'I'll be at the jailhouse. I'll stay there until I got all the money. Anythin' more gents?'

When the meeting broke up and men appeared past the closed drapery the saloon became as quiet as a grave. Of the palavers only one remained inside. That was Clancy Harney who did not intend to pay a substitute barman any more than he had to.

For the marshal it had been a long, tiring day. He locked up across the road and went up to the rooming-house to bed down. Some idiot was playing a mouth harp, badly. Boyle went to the door in his stockinged feet and yelled out that if the musician didn't stop his racket, Boyle would come to his room, kick in the door and use one of the slats to brain him.

It was the kind of remark, made in a booming, angry voice, that would have kept even Beethoven quiet for the rest of the night.

The following morning there was a high, thin overcast which partially obscured the sun which, in at least one way was a blessing; an obscured sun would be unable to make life miserable with heat, at least until the overcast burned off.

Marshal Boyle arrived at the café at the worst possible time for someone with things on his mind; he did not want to talk with other diners at the counter. He ordered breakfast in a surly growl, which inhibited the diners seated on both sides of him but which went unheard by an old cowman farther down where the counter curved into the wall. This rough-looking individual called to the marshal. 'Folks're talkin' Mister Boyle. Seems there's In'ians back in the country.'

The lawman glared at the stockroom and dourly said, 'Is that a fact!'

The cowman went silent, so did the other diners several of whom finished eating quickly and departed. By the time Boyle also finished, arose to toss coins on the counter, he was almost alone at the counter.

Over in the jailhouse he made a small, dry-wood fire, put the coffee pot in place and went to his desk to sit down and lean back. Mister Hammond came over from the store well before noon with his $2000 dollars in a cloth sack which he dropped on the lawman's desk, sat down and said, 'Jim Murphy's share is in there too even though he ain't showed up yet to sign the note.'

Boyle eyed the little sack. 'It's early. He's got chores to do.'

Hammond seemed not to have heard.

'Marshal, it ain't right what them In'ians is doin' to folks in Martindale.'

'I expect, Mister Hammond, that'd depend on whether you own a store in town, or own the land, wouldn't it?'

Hammond ignored the remark to add more to what he'd said, but he did not say it until he was in the doorway with the latch in his hand. 'If Corey Kincade was around things would get settled different.'

After the door closed the marshal opened the cloth bag, counted the greenbacks, tugged the pucker string closed and sat like a statue for several moments before stowing the sack in a drawer and heading for the door.

He didn't get outside; Clancy met him with a rumpled envelope which he handed over as he said, 'It'd help, if you was to get in writin' that those In'ians'll never come back.'

Boyle accepted the bulky envelope while gazing at the saloonman. 'It would be nice, Clancy, but I got an idea the only one of 'em who could write is Hugh Black, an' I doubt like hell that he'd oblige. Is the full two thousand in here?'

'All of it in greenbacks. That leaves me with eighty-seven dollars in my savings.' Boyle was not touched.

'How much would it cost to rebuild your saloon if you got burnt out?'

Clancy crossed to the front of the emporium, turned left and hiked up to his place of business. Like the others, it hurt to part with that much money; also like the others it left him feeling robbed.

Boyle went grudgingly to the corralyard. Old Jake led the way to his office. The empty safe had its door hanging open. Someone had replaced the company papers and ledger books where they belonged but the interior tin drawer used for storing money was broken and dented. It had been placed atop the safe.

Jake pointed to a chair, sat down at his untidy desk and glared. 'You know I'm agin' this.'

Boyle nodded. He had anticipated this and sat in silence like an oversized expressionless buddha.

'The telegraph line's been fixed so I

wired Denver this morning about what happened. They won't like it.'

Boyle said, 'No one likes it, Jake. Did you explain to Denver you couldn't help what happened?'

'Of course, but that won't make much difference. Up there folks ain't interested in anythin' except how much is left over after expenses. An' I had to tell 'em how much we was robbed of. There'll be federal marshals down here quicker'n you can say scat. Seems to me you hadn't ought to be settin' there. You should have a posse mounted an' armed to go up there and bury them savages. My company'll wonder about that.'

Boyle left the corralyard heading for the opposite end of town, down where Andy Sears had his smithy. When he got down there the blacksmith handed him a small leather pouch which he'd been carrying tucked under his shoeing apron. Sears made an exaggerated sigh and rolled his eyes. 'It ain't like Mister Hammond's store. Down here I sweat'n ache for every dollar.'

Jim Murphy came over from the livery barn. From his expression it would be safe to figure he'd been dragged through a knothole. He barely looked at Boyle and Sears as he sat on a a little horseshoe keg. The blacksmith said, 'You sick, Jim?'

Murphy shook his head. 'Not that medicine'd help. You want to see the note I had to sign for Mister Hammond?'

Neither the lawman or the blacksmith spoke.

Murphy sat slumped. 'He loaned me two thousand dollars. I had to sign his paper to repay at six percent interest within thirty days. I can't do it.'

Sears said, 'Did you tell him that?'

'Yes, an' you know what he said? He can't extend the note. I'm goin' to lose my stock, my wagons an' my barn.' Murphy looked up. 'I wish I'd never seen this damned country.'

Marshal Boyle left the smithy, hiked up as far as the emporium and was told by the clerk that Mister Hammond wouldn't be back until the following morning, and no, he had no idea where he had gone.

Boyle was at the jailhouse counting the money he had collected when the preacher walked in, got owl-eyed at the sight of all those greenbacks, sat down and seemed to be waiting for some kind of explanation, which he did not get, so he said, 'There's some kind of feathered ornament hanging on the tombstone of His Horse Is Black.'

Marshal Boyle leaned back. What had been said the previous night in Clancy's card room was evidently correct. Tomahawks could sneak around in darkness like ghosts.

Reverend Severn studied the large man for several moments then arose. Marshal Boyle was clearly a long way from Martindale in his thoughts.

At the door Severn said, 'Should I leave that In'ian thing on the stone?'

Boyle replied dryly, 'It's better'n black paint, Preacher.'

'I'd like to know who put it there an' why. There haven't been In'ians around in years.'

Marshal Boyle smiled bleakly. 'There are In'ians around, Reverend. I'd leave the ornament where it is.'

After the minister left Marshal Boyle went over to the café after locking the ransom money in his small office safe.

He was early, there were three other men at the counter. One of them Jake Miller. He would not look at the marshal nor speak to him.

Normally a hearty feeder, this day the marshal had almost no appetite. When he made a cursory round of the town as was his normal custom, he was buttonholed by the telegrapher, Ulysses S. Beaver, who seemed to want to speak very privately so they stepped into a dogtrot between two buildings and the wiry man with the blue eyeshade spoke swiftly and quietly. 'Somethin's goin' on, Marshal. Us telegraphers take an oath never to talk about what we transmit nor receive. But this is different. Did you ever hear of a man called Sloan Dalton?'

Boyle's eyes widened. The name of Sloan Dalton could be found on Wanted posters from Montana to Texas. There was no more notorious outlaw west of the Missouri.

Boyle said, 'What about him?'

'He's comin' to Martindale.'

'How do you know that?'

'That's what I'm gettin' at—but you got to pass me your solemn word you won't never repeat anythin' I tell you.'

Boyle promised.

'You know that old man lives in that tumbledown hotel at the lower end of town, the one they call old Abner?'

Boyle nodded.

'Well, he sent a telegram to Tonopah for Sloan Dalton to come to Martindale as fast as he can get here.'

The marshal scowled. 'It was addressed to Sloan Dalton?'

'Yes sir, plain as day.'

'Mister Beaver, Sloan Dalton operates in a lot of places an' he's got rewards on him until hell freezes over. Now tell me, you think he'd be in Tonopah usin' his right name?'

The wizened man sniffled, ran a threadbare cuff under his nose and said, 'All's

I'm tellin' you is gospel truth. If you want come to my office an' I'll show you the telegram to Sloan Dalton over at Tonopah.'

As the wiry man turned to lead the way Marshal Boyle caught him by the arm. 'Who sent the telegram?' he asked.

'I told you. That scarecrow who lives down yonder, the one named Abner Holt.'

Marshal Boyle gave the smaller man a slight push and followed him to the telegraph office. The telegrapher peeked out his roadway window, picked up a yellow paper and shoved the lawman toward a tiny storeroom as he said, 'I can't have no passerby seein' you in here readin' telegrams.'

There was no light in the stuffy small room but there was a window. Boyle read the telegram twice, came out of the little room, tossed the yellow paper on the telegrapher's desk and left the wireless office walking south.

# 8

## The Interim

Old Abner was digging in soil as hard as stone out behind the old hotel when the marshal found him. He straightened up with a groan, shook his head and said, 'Whoever said the Lord done a good job when he engineered folks didn't know what he was talkin' about. Ten minutes peckin' in this dirt an' my back's killin' me.'

The lawman neither agreed nor disagreed about the Lord's handiwork; he faced the rawboned older man as solemn as a judge and said, 'You know Sloan Dalton?'

Abner leaned on his shovel gazing dispassionately at the lawman. 'Never seen him in my life.'

'How did you know he was in Tonopah?'

The dispassionate gaze brightened slightly. 'Oh that. The danged screwt ain't supposed

138

to let folks read telegrams.'

Marshal Boyle lied with a clear conscience. 'He didn't let me read it. It was lyin' on his table an' I saw it. Now, tell me again you don't know Dalton.'

'I don't. Like I said, I never seen him in my life, that I know of anyway. I got to set down.'

Marshal Boyle waited until the old man was seated then said, 'Your name was on the telegram.'

Abner eased back against the building and sighed. 'I got paid a silver dollar for sendin' it. He give me the name 'n where to send it.'

'Who did?'

'Marshal, a man's got to respect the privacy of other folks. I was told that when I warn't more'n knee high to a horse.'

Marshal Boyle also leaned back. They were in shade but as the spring had turned to summer heat increased. 'Abner, I got a notion to lock you up an' go horseback ridin' for a couple of days. No food an' no water.'

'Mister Hammond. He had to leave

town. He wanted the telegram sent right away an' give me a cartwheel for sendin' it.'

Marshal Boyle tipped down his hat and squinted into the distance. He was quiet so long old Abner leaned to arise and go back to his digging. 'Got to get some beans'n whatnot planted,' he said.

Marshal Boyle eyed the *caliche*. 'Nothin' but weeds'll grow in that ground, Abner. What did he say about Sloan Dalton?'

'Nothin'. He was in a hurry to catch the stage. He give me a piece of paper with the message an' the address. That's all. Except for the silver dollar. So I hiked up yonder an... You ever hear of a scrawny turkey like that telegrapher bein' named after Gen'ral Grant?'

Marshal Boyle returned to the jailhouse, sat down and wagged his head. Hammond? Marshal Boyle had never liked the man. It wasn't anything he could put his finger on.

Sloan Dalton in Tonopah? Using his own name when he was wanted in at least two territories and three states for

140

everything from murder to bank and train robbery?

He returned to the emporium, leaned on the counter until the clerk had cared for a customer, then asked again where Mister Hammond had gone, and got the same answer again. 'I don't know. All he told me was that he had business to attend to, that he might be gone until tomorrow.'

Boyle went up to the stage office and asked old Jake if he knew which coach Mister Hammond had left on. Jake snarled, 'Of course I know. I run this business don't I?'

'Which one, Jake?'

'The last stage yestiddy evenin' north-bound.'

'Did he say where he was goin'?'

'Why should he tell me? Just pay the fare, be here when the rig leaves an' a passenger can be on his way to hell for all I care.'

There were several towns north of Martindale. Hammond could change coaches at any one of them which meant he could have restaged east or west. He returned to the jailhouse and Hugh Black appeared in the doorway. Boyle neither smiled nor nodded. 'I got most of the money,' he said. 'Can't get the rest for another day or so.'

Black did not leave the doorway. 'Show me what you got,' he said, and Boyle reddened as he went to the little safe, opened it, removed the pouches and emptied them atop his desk.

'You figured I was lyin' did you?'

Black considered the pile of greenbacks as he replied, 'No. They're gettin' restless up yonder. Now I can go back an' say I saw it. One thing, Marshal, come along when you bring it up yonder.'

'The feller who runs the saloon will come with me.'

Hugh Black smiled lightly. 'Folks think you might run off with the money, do they?'

Boyle stood at his desk with clenched fists. 'Mister, some day—'

'You got until day after tomorrow,' Hugh Black said, and left the doorway.

Boyle returned the money to the pouches

142

and locked them in the safe, then leaned there while a dark thought crossed his mind. Those damned tomahawks had busted Jake's safe which was larger and more formidable than the jailhouse safe.

He opened the safe, took the pouches out, closed the safe and pondered. Hiding the pouches in the jailhouse would be fine except that the jailhouse was a bare-bones establishment.

He decided to carry the pouches with him.

The only salutary thing thus far was that he had two more full days to finish what he had to do.

He returned to the corralyard, entered Jake's office and got welcomed with a sound like a spitting cat. The disagreeable stager held up a hand. 'I've pondered on it, Marshal. Not a gawddamned red cent do them savages get out'n me. They already robbed the company.'

Boyle sat down, leaned back and stonily eyed the cranky soul opposite him. 'All right. But let me tell you somethin'. When they burn the town because we come up

143

short I'm goin' to make a point of seein' that folks know why. Because you wouldn't kick in like the other done. You know what they'll do to you, Jake? Hang you.'

'You threatenin' me, Marshal?'

'Nope,' the large man replied, and arose looking down at the wizened man at the cluttered desk. 'You got until mornin' to change your mind.' Boyle went to the door and spoke with one hand on the latch. 'Jake, I've told you a dozen times to have your whips walk their teams half a mile from the outskirts of town. Folks complain about the dust. From today on every whip that raises dust gets locked up.'

'What! That ain't no crime!'

'Disturbin' the peace is. Somethin' else, Jake; before a whip leaves town on one of your stages he's to come to the jailhouse.'

'What for?'

'So I can smell his breath. No driver leaves town that's had a drink.'

Jake sprang up from the desk glaring, bony hands curled into fists. 'You can't do that. The town council's got to make regulations like that.'

'The council will, I promise you. An' one other thing, Jake, Andy can't shoe any of your horses from now on unless I've gone over each animal.'

'I keep good care of my stock an' you know it.'

'One windpuff, one sore shoulder, one cut or collar sore.'

'You idiot, there ain't a horse alive past six years that don't have a windpuff. They don't mean nothin'!'

Marshal Boyle stepped out, closed the door and went down to the smithy to explain to Andy Sears what he had told Jake, and why he had done it.

Sears stood in thought for a moment before speaking. 'The stage company is my bread'n butter, Marshal.'

Boyle nodded about that. 'We're maybe two thousand shy, Andy. You want to ante up another five hundred, because that'll be about your share if Jake don't bring me his two thousand.'

The blacksmith was silent for another moment before speaking again. 'I don't have no five hunnert dollars. Maybe Mister

Hammond has an' maybe Clancy has, but Jim Murphy don't an' neither do I.'

'Clancy cleaned out his savings, Andy, to make his two thousand, so that well is dry too. Your share might run a tad more'n five hundred.'

The blacksmith exploded. 'I've a notion to skin that old son of a bitch alive.'

'You wouldn't get more'n fifty cents for the hide.'

'I'm goin' up there and pound some sense into him, so help me.'

Marshal Boyle shrugged and left the smithy. Across the road Jim Murphy was sitting on an ancient bench in front of his livery barn. As the lawman crossed over Murphy raised his head. 'I'm goin' out to California,' he said.

Marshal Boyle sat down. 'What's out there?'

'What's here?' Murphy said bitterly. 'I been buildin' up my business for years. Marshal, you really think them In'ians'd burn the town?'

'They've burnt other towns, Jim. Old Jake refuses to ante up his share.'

Murphy straightened up on the bench. 'They'd burn him out too, don't he know that?'

'He don't own the corralyard, his office, the outbuildings. He don't even own the horses.'

Murphy slowly reddened. He leaned to peer around the lawman northward in the direction of the corralyard. He slowly resumed his former position. He did not speak, did not appear aware of the large man on the same bench.

Marshal Boyle left the liveryman sitting there gazing straight ahead. At the jailhouse Boyle stood briefly by the small, barred front window before going to his desk. The noisy ones like Andy Sears were predictable. The sombre ones like Jim Murphy were not.

A short while later he heard the noisy arrival of Jake's afternoon coach at the upper end of town and went to watch. Sure enough, the whip loped his horses almost to the entrance to the corralyard before hauling them down to a walk. Dust trailed the rig.

Marshal Boyle did not hasten as he hiked northward. Several strangers off the stage were fanning out from the corralyard.

When the marshal entered the yard the whip, a wiry, short man known as Smitty Haldane was tucking his smoke-tanned gauntlets under his belt. His back was to the lawman. In front of the whip Jake was speaking. He abruptly stopped talking. He was looking over Haldane's shoulder, the same shoulder Marshal Boyle spun the driver around by with his right hand while he emptied Haldane's hip-holster with his left hand.

The whip's jaw dropped, his normally squinty eyes widened. Marshal Boyle said, 'Dust, Smitty. You know there's an ordnance about coaches comin' into town raisin' dust.'

Haldane was still too stunned to speak as Marshal Boyle herded him from the corralyard down to the jailhouse. Behind them Jake Miller approached in the gateway hopping from foot to foot. Before turning back into the yard he violently shook his fist in the marshal's direction.

He snapped at his yardmen and stamped all the way to his office, where the town blacksmith was standing, having entered through the roadway door.

Jake said, 'What do you want!'

Sears didn't raise his voice. 'I want you to tell me you ain't goin' to pitch in your share for the In'ians, an' when you tell me that I'm goin' to half kill you with my hands!'

Jake stood behind his desk, shaking with anger. Opposite him was an unsmiling, muscular man whose expression said volumes.

Jake sank down at the desk, fished in a drawer until he found his snuff, got a fair-sized pinch tucked between his lip and his gum, put the little box away, closed the drawer and said, 'Give me one reason why I should let them tomahawks hold me up.'

'I'll give you two reasons, Jake. The first one is that from what I've heard you was in on havin' that old In'ian killed. The second reason is that if you don't chip in, I'm goin' to break half the bones in your damned body!'

Jake spluttered. 'It wasn't me. It was Arthur Hammond had him killed.'

'Are you goin' to chip in or not? The rest of us have, an' it's like to ruin us.'

'How do I explain it to the company in Denver? Two thousand dollars is—'

'Jake,' the blacksmith said, as he crossed to the front of the desk. 'The rest of us don't give a damn about your bosses in Denver. Tell 'em anythin' you want to or tell 'em nothin', but right now you tell me whether you're going to chip in or not. *Right damned now!*'

'Andy, for Chris'sake they already got their money from the safe. You don't expect me to chip in another two thousand. That'd be more'n—'

'Jake, the In'ian said two thousand from each of us. He never said nothin' about includin' what he got from your safe. That was your idea. Now, we're two thousand shy of what he told us he wants. That money he got from your safe belonged to the stage company.'

Jake looked up sharply. 'Are you sayin' I got to personally put up two thousand?'

150

'Only unless you want to get broke up so bad you'll spend the rest of your life in a damned bed! Jake, I'm through talkin'!'

Jake Miller was many things but a fool was not among them. 'I don't have that much money in my pocket,' he told the blacksmith.

'You got it at the bank?'

'Yes.'

'I'll set here an' wait. An' Jake, don't try anythin' that'll upset me.'

'Like what?'

'Like goin' after the marshal. This here is just between you'n me.' Andy Sears returned to the chair he had vacated and sat down.

Jake Miller arose, stood behind his desk considering the blacksmith, mumbled something profane and stamped out of the office.

The blacksmith shoved out oaken legs, considered the scuffed toes of his boots and only raised his eyes when Jim Murphy came past the corralyard doorway and stopped dead still at the sight of Andy Sears.

After the moment of surprise passed, the liveryman said, 'Where is he?'

'Jake? He went up to the bank. Why?'

'What'd he go to the bank for?' Murphy asked, and got a short reply.

'For two thousand dollars, his share of what we need for that tomahawk.'

Murphy leaned on the wall studying Sears. 'For a fact, Andy?'

Sears nodded. 'I'm waitin' for him to return. Set down, you wait too.'

The liveryman found a rickety chair, eased down and looked around. 'You threaten him, did you?' he asked, without looking at the blacksmith.

'Not exactly, Jim. I made him a promise. If he didn't kick in like the rest of us done I'd overhaul him from hell to breakfast.'

In the yard someone was loudly cursing a stubborn mule and another yardman laughed. 'He don't know what you're sayin'. You got to cuss Messican mules in Spanish.'

The angry hostler replied angrily, 'I'll shoot the son of a bitch!'

The other hostler spoke sharply. 'Drop

the shank. Now then, let me show you somethin'. Don't never face a mule when you want to lead 'em. You can't drag somethin' that weighs nine hunnert pounds an' mules don't like folks starin' 'em in the face an' yellin' at 'em.'

For a moment there was silence then the irate yardman said, 'I'll be damned. Where'd you learn about mules?'

'In Missouri where they got more mules than trees. Now, just let the shank play out from your hand an' walk ahead of him. That's it. Good.'

The man who had laughed had one more piece of advice which he presented sarcastically. 'I can't believe you been around livestock as long as you said. Slade, you can't even lead a horse while you're facin' him let alone a mule.'

Someone entered the office from the roadway entrance. Both Murphy and Sears looked up expecting Jake Miller. The newcomer was Marshal Boyle. He eyed them, held up a small buckskin pouch and jerked his head. They followed him outside where Jake was waiting. When he would have spoken Boyle held up a warning hand, turned and herded the liveryman and the blacksmith in the direction of the jailhouse.

Down there he upended the leather pouch, sorted through the double eagles, and finally spoke. He did not scold, but he was reproachful, particularly toward the blacksmith.

'You hadn't ought to have scairt the whey out of old Jake.'

Andy Sears sat on a bench. 'He said he'd fetch the money.'

'He did,' stated the lawman. 'There it is, but he was scairt of goin' back to his office because he said you figured to maim him.'

'To what?'

'Hurt him, put him down with busted bones.'

Jim Murphy went to the door, opened it, looked out, hung there a long moment then turned his face toward the lawman. 'Mister Hammond's over yonder talkin' to a 'breed In'ian.'

Boyle scooped the money back into its

pouch, pocketed the bag and brushed past the two men on his way across the road. Sears and Murphy went out front, stood in shade and watched. The blacksmith made the only comment either of them made when he said, 'That ain't one of them broncos from up yonder. All of a sudden we got In'ians comin' out'n our ears.'

# 9

## The Surprise

The storekeeper reacted nervously to the approach of the marshal. He said something brusque and the swarthy stranger walked northward without looking back.

Mister Hammond smiled as Boyle stepped up on to the duck boards. The marshal had never been a tactful individual. He nodded in the direction of the dark man as he said, 'Who's he?'

Hammond looked northward as he replied. 'Messican I met on the stage. I don't recollect his name.' Hammond seemed to gain confidence from the sound of his own voice. He faced the marshal and smiled again. 'Anythin' happen while I was gone?'

Marshal Boyle watched the swarthy man enter Clancy's saloon when he replied.

'Nothin' much. Jake come through with his money.'

'You got it all?'

Boyle nodded. 'I'll take it up yonder in the morning.'

'Alone?'

'No. Clancy wants to ride along.'

The Marshal wanted the worst way to ask where Mister Hammond had gone but could not think of a way of asking, and being pointblank would not sit well with Mister Hammond. But he had something to enquire about, and perhaps inadvertently he was tactful when he said, 'I set a spell with Abner Holt yesterday.'

Hammond's smile winked out. He gazed steadily at the lawman waiting for what came next. It wasn't much of a wait.

'I can understand someone bein' in a hurry to catch a stage. How did you know Sloan Dalton was in the area?'

Hammond fidgeted with the gold chain across his middle. 'Sloan Dalton the outlaw?' he said, and Boyle neither answered nor took his eyes off the storekeeper. Hammond said, 'It was a

157

joke. An old friend of mine over in Tonopah knew Dalton yeas ago. I was just havin' a little fun.'

'You sent a telegram to your friend usin' the name of a wanted outlaw? How do you expect that to set with the law over there?'

'Well, like I said, it was a joke. I never met Dalton, got no idea where he is. I just wanted to...'

'Mister Hammond, the telegram said for Dalton to come to Martindale in a hurry.'

Hammond nodded. 'That was part of the joke, Marshal.'

Boyle considered the heavy man thoughtfully. 'Don't you ever play a joke on me, Mister Hammond.'

The storekeeper waited until the lawman was back across the road then hot-footed it in the direction of the saloon. Boyle watched this from his little barred roadway window.

Later, he went down to the smithy, got a cool greeting from Sears and asked pointblank if Andy would accompany him and Clancy in the morning to give the Indians the money. Sears considered a long moment before nodding. 'You got a reason for wantin' an escort, Marshal.'

'I'll tell you when we're on our way.'

The blacksmith went back to work and missed seeing the lawman cross to Murphy's barn where he asked the same question and got the same response. Jim Murphy would ride with the marshal to the old rancheria at first light the following morning.

He turned Smitty Haldane loose, admonished him about raising dust when he drove into town and would have sent him on his way except that the whip said, 'Jake's a real pain in the butt. He told me that ordnance about dust didn't matter.'

'Now you know better,' Boyle replied tartly.

'Last time I hauled Mister Hammond he told me the town council's facin' trouble with some tomahawks an' he figures to straighten it out.'

After the whip departed Marshal Boyle went to his little barred window and gazed in the direction of the general store. He was beginning to suspect something unpleasant.

He went up to Clancy's place and asked about a dark stranger. Clancy nodded. 'He was in here a while back. Drank whiskey like he had cast-iron insides.'

'Did he talk?'

'Well, he said he never even heard of Martindale before an' it's got too many people.'

'Did he mention Mister Hammond?'

'Nope, but he said he figured to come back to Martindale in a day or so, then forget he ever seen the place.' Clancy studied the lawman. 'Is something wrong?'

'I'm not sure. Clancy, meet me at Murphy's barn at daybreak and fetch your Winchester.'

After the marshal went past the swinging doors Clancy leaned on his bar gazing after him. One thing he had learned about the big man was that he didn't waste words. Clancy had to find his fill-in barman because he did not expect to return to town until late the following day, and that annoyed him because he had to pay a half-dollar to the stand-in barman.

He didn't see Marshal Boyle for the rest of the day. Boyle didn't even show up for his customary night-cap.

Jake Miller arrived early when the saloon was empty because its normal patrons were at supper. Clancy got a bottle and glass and rolled his eyes heavenward when the old stager said, 'You know what that danged town marshal done? I can't send out a driver until the marshal's smelt his breath. An' that ain't all. He said Andy couldn't shoe no more horses until he said it would be all right, an' the big tub of guts locked Smitty up for raisin' dust. I tell you, Clancy, he's gettin' awful hard to live with.'

The saloonman had a question. 'What'd you do, Jake? He don't normally come down hard on folks.'

'I don't want to talk about it. Did you make this rot-gut? You got nerve to expect a nickel for a drink of this siwash, Clancy.'

Harney ignored the last remark. 'I'm

goin' with him tomorrow when he takes the money up yonder.'

The whiskey may have been bad but that did not prevent old Jake from refilling his glass as he said, 'This town's crazy. In the old days we'd have made up a posse and gone after them broncos like a herd of cougars. Gawda'mighty, Clancy, this here ain't whiskey, it's embalmin' fluid. Taste it.'

Clancy shook his head. 'I don't drink'n work at the same time. All right, Jake, keep your money.'

The old man left the saloon in the same foul mood he'd been in when he entered.

The following morning just shy of first light they met at Murphy's barn. As they were rigging out, Smitty Haldane, the stage driver, walked in leading a goat-eyed, roman-nosed big sorrel horse that had muscle where most horses didn't even have the place for it. He was wearing his sheep-pelt coat and had a booted saddlegun in place under the right-side rosadero of his saddle. At the owlish looks he got he smiled and said, 'Jake

162

was hoppin' mad. I'm supposed to take out the relay from up north. He fired me.'

Marshal Boyle said, 'What are you doin' here?'

'Figured you could use another posse rider.'

Boyle let reins slip through his fingers as he faced the stager. 'How did you know we'd be riding?'

'Mister Hammond told me yestiddy evenin' you'd most likely head out for that In'ian meadow up yonder first thing this mornin'. Look; I got guns enough if there's trouble.'

Jim Murphy snorted. 'All we're goin' to do is ride up there, give 'em the money an' come back.'

Smitty Haldane was a wiry, friendly individual, one of those people it was hard not to like, even on empty stomachs. The caféman wouldn't fire up his cookstove nor fog his windows for an hour or more, by which time Marshal Boyle and his companions were well clear of town, heads tucked low inside turned-up coat collars, silent as mutes.

Marshal Boyle led the way through the poor light of a dying night. It had been his intention to reach the uplands, the foothills at least, before sunrise, and while he didn't quite made it visibility was limited even after dawn's first glow appeared.

He stopped with a forested background, turned and studied the country they had traversed. It was flat to rolling with occasional arroyos.

It was empty. There were not even any cattle out of their beds to graze. Clancy leaned on his saddlehorn. 'You expectin' somethin'?' he asked and the marshal shrugged in silence and lifted his rein hand to resume the ride when Smitty Haldane stopped him. 'Look yonder. That bitch coyote's runnin' like her life depended on it.'

The coyote was of a colour that blended. Except for her movement they would not have seen her.

Andy Sears back-tracked her with squinted eyes as he said, 'It wasn't us that spooked her. We rode past an' she never paid no attention. Marshal, see that jumble of big rocks easterly? That's where she come from.'

They followed the blacksmith's direction, sat in silence studying the boulder field until Smitty Haldane said, 'It could have been a cougar or maybe a dog-coyote on the peck.'

No one heeded Haldane's remark. That bitch coyote was running with her belly hair skimming the ground.

Andy leaned, squinty eyed. 'It's in them rocks, whatever it is.'

Marshal Boyle, silent until now, dryly said, 'Lads, I'm carryin' a fortune in sound money. I figured somethin' might come up.'

Sears nodded without looking away from the field of big rocks. 'This takes me back some years,' he said quietly. 'When I was younger folks watched their back trail, specially in tomahawk country.' Sears straightened up in the saddle looking at the marshal. 'Suppose, we spread out wide, pass the rocks an' come in from behind 'em.'

Boyle leaned to expectorate before

nodding. This was what had worried him since he'd told Mister Hammond he'd be taking the money to the rancheria. All he said was, 'Ride with your guns in your lap,' and kneed his horse into motion.

Jim Murphy shook his head. The ground to be covered did not have a clump of brush nor a tree, it was flat to rolling with an occasional gully. Before widening the distance between himself and Marshal Boyle he said, 'If it's men in them rocks they can see everything we do.'

The marshal did not reply. That same notion was in the back of his mind. They were sitting targets. As daylight increased visibility became perfect, and Boyle's much earlier suspicion began to crystalize. Half the outlaws west of the Big Muddy would ask nothing better than an even chance to rob someone of $10,000.

When Murphy was wide to the south and Sears was an equal distance northward, Marshal Boyle moved at a steady walk until he was almost in hand-gun range, then halted. He sat for a long time gazing in the direction of the big rocks. If there was movement he did not detect it, and it crossed his mind that if what they were stalking turned out to be a rutting dog-coyote he'd never hear the end of it.

A man arose behind some rocks, they protected him from the waist down. He was holding a saddle gun in both hands. Marshal Boyle called to him. 'Good morning.'

The man did not reply.

Marshal Boyle, with his six-gun in his lap, eased the horse ahead another few yards. Northward, the blacksmith was passing down the side of the boulder field. To the south the liveryman was doing the same. They evidently had not seen the man arise facing the lawman.

Boyle halted when he was close enough to make out the swarthy features of the stranger. He called again, with less force this time. 'I'm Town Marshal Boyle from Martindale.'

That's as far as he got, two men came over the lip of a shallow arroyo with Winchesters held at the ready. Boyle looked for the blacksmith; he should have seen the men in the arroyo but clearly he hadn't.

Finally, the man protected by rocks spoke. He had no accent but clearly he was either a Mexican or a 'breed Indian. He said, 'That money you got—drop it!'

Boyle made no move to obey. 'What money?'

The swarthy man flared out in anger. 'The gawddamned money that was raised in Martindale to buy off some In'ians. Mister, we been waitin' for you since last night. *Drop the money!*'

Sears and Murphy were sitting stone still to the north and south where armed men had arisen among the rocks to face them.

Marshal Boyle said, 'All right. I got it in pouches inside my shirt.'

The dark man placed his Winchester atop a rock which protected him but did not cock it. He was impatiently waiting for the lawman to shed the pouches. As Boyle started to unbutton his shirt he said, 'You'll never make it, mister.'

'We'll make it, drop the damned money!'

'Did he tell you what the money was for?'

'Some In'ians.'

Boyle dropped one sack, held the second one in his hand as he said, 'Mister, they been watchin' the trail since we showed up on it. They'll see what's happenin' here.'

'Just shed them pouches you windy old bastard. No In'ians'll catch us. Hurry up!'

Marshal Boyle did not hurry as he gradually divested himself of all the small pouches. When he said, 'That's all,' the dark man snarled; 'Take your coat off an' your shirt.'

Boyle obeyed again, without haste. When he was naked from the waist up the swarthy man pursed his lips. Marshal Boyle without his shirt looked even more formidable than he looked wearing a shirt.

The dark man did not take his eyes off the lawman when he raised his voice slightly.

A youngster, no more than twelve or fourteen years of age, clambered out of the rocks, made a beeline for the pouches without once looking up at the large man atop the large horse.

169

When he scuttled back among the rocks the dark man growled at him until the youngster was no longer in sight, then he faced the marshal again and started to speak when a keening high scream, blood-curdling in its intensity, stopped the dark man with his mouth open.

He looked from left to right, faced Boyle again and said, 'Shed your pistol an' come into the rocks. Damn it, move!'

In the middle distance both Andy Sears and Jim Murphy had dismounted and swung their horses sideways with each of them on the far side. The men farther back with Winchesters acted frightened by that scream. They sank low trying to locate its source.

Boyle did the same as he dismounted. If there had been more than one scream its origin could have been placed, but it had only sounded once and its aftermath had upset the men in the rocks.

When Marshal Boyle scooped up his shirt and coat before climbing among the rocks, the swarthy man said, 'Where are they!'

Boyle answered calmly. 'Everywhere. All around you.'

'There's only four or five of 'em,' the dark man exclaimed, and again the lawman replied quietly. 'He lied to you. I don't know why unless it's because he wants you to get killed.'

'How many?' the agitated dark man demanded.

Boyle lied with a clear conscience. 'Sixteen.'

'How do you know that?'

'We met up at their old rancheria. That's how many I counted.'

'Who'n hell are they?'

'In'ians, mister. Hold-outs'n renegades. They don't take prisoners.'

The swarthy man was briefly distracted by a 'breed Indian who came up to say, 'Challo, we can't run for it until we know where they are.'

The swarthy man offered an angry retort. 'They wasn't supposed to be out of their mountains.'

'But they are, Challo.'

The other man, short with tan-tawny

eyes and a light complexion scowled. 'You don't see In'ians unless they want you to see 'em. You know that. How many are there?'

Challo replied irritably. 'How would I know? This lawman says there is sixteen of 'em.'

The 'breed eyes widened. 'That's too many.'

'Not as long as we keep to the rocks an' don't let 'em get in here.'

'Challo! You're talkin' crazy. Five of us against sixteen In'ians we can't even see. Palaver. Talk; kill time. Give 'em the damned money. Challo, my brothers 'n me don't aim to lose our hair. Not over no damned money.'

As the 'breed turned away Marshal Boyle said, 'It might work. They might palaver.'

Challo glared. 'Give 'em the money?'

'It belongs to 'em anyway.'

The swarthy man put a sly look on the lawman. 'Put your shirt on. Do you know 'em well enough so's they won't shoot you?'

'I think so.'

'Get on your horse, find 'em and make 'em an offer, half the money.'

As Boyle was climbing out of the rock field one of the renegades called to him.

'Where you goin'?'

'To palaver.'

The renegade nodded. 'Keep 'em talkin' mister, and maybe you'll come out alive.'

Marshal Boyle walked to his horse, leaned briefly across the saddle seat, saw no one, swung astride and walked his horse in a northerly direction toward the arroyo where those two men had appeared with carbines. He had not seen them again, nor did he believe they had left the gully and got among the rocks where their companions were sweating.

It was a good guess, or maybe it wasn't but he had been seen riding in that direction and the watchers had moved to intercept him. In any case as he halted near the lip of the arroyo a quiet voice said, 'Get off. Lead your horse down here.'

Marshal Boyle obeyed.

It was hot, the sun had been climbing

steadily. In the arroyo with no shade and with no way for the occasional breeze to get down there, it was even hotter.

Hugh Black's shirtfront was dark, he flung off sweat as he spoke to the marshal. 'We saw you comin'. Who are them men in the rocks?'

Boyle leaned in the shade of his horse. 'First, I'll tell you what they want—half the money.'

An Indian standing nearby snorted.

'I'm not sure who they are but I saw one of them in town yesterday, an' the man he was talkin' to—as sure as I'm standin' here—hired them to catch me before I got to the meadow an' take the money.'

'You got it, Marshal?'

'I had it. They got it now.'

Hugh Black glanced where his companions were impassively standing. One of them said something in a gruff voice that the marshal did not understand.

Hugh Black considered the lawman. 'Are you thirsty?'

'I could spit cotton.'

He spoke to the dour, gruff man in the

same language. The Indian took a gut pouch from a man who held it out, gave it to Black who handed it to the marshal.

Tepid water carried in an animal intestine left something to be desired unless a man was as thirsty as Marshal Boyle was. He drank deeply, handed back the pouch and muttered, 'Thanks.'

Black ignored that and asked how many men were in the rocks. Marshal Boyle spat aside before answering. 'Five that I saw.'

Hugh Black nodded. 'We got a long wait. Until night.'

Boyle shook his head. 'I'm supposed to keep you palaverin'. That means they figure to run for it. You wait until dark an' you'll lose 'em.'

The dour, gruff Indian spoke again in that guttural, slightly sing-song language. Black listened, spoke to the other men in the same language then faced the marshal. 'You go back. Tell them we're goin' to council. If we decide to take half I'll wave a blanket.' Black showed a faint, humourless smile. 'We'll see who kills time palaverin'.'

Boyle moved to mount as he said, 'They won't wait long. They're scairt and scairt men do foolish things.'

'Go back,' Hugh Black told the marshal, which the lawman did, riding up out of the arroyo at a slow walk, a gait he did not increase the full distance back to the rocks where the man called Challo was waiting with several other renegades.

The liveryman and blacksmith were still in place using their animals as shields. No one seemed interested in them, only in the marshal.

# 10

## Complications

When Marshal Boyle told Challo and the renegades around him what the Indians had said, no one was pleased and the 'breed with goat-like tan eyes cursed before saying, 'Let 'em council. Challo we got to get away from here, In'ians or no In'ians.'

The dark man replied irritably. 'How, you fool, make a run for it broad daylight?'

'Why not?' one of the other renegades asked.

'Five of us scatterin' like quail in open country, an' sixteen of them tomahawks chasin' us?' Challo scowled in contempt for his companions who had urged immediate flight.

The youngest among them who was noteworthy for wearing a pair of crossed bandoleers, piped up in a voice that was on the verge of changing. He had the same goat-coloured eyes as another of the renegades. They were brothers. The youngster said 'We done it before an' got away with it.'

The older man regarded the youth. One of them said, 'Done what?'

'Snuck in an' run off their horses.'

The older men did not say a word. When they resumed palavering they completely ignored the youngster.

A weathered, grey and older man said, 'Give 'em half the money. We ain't goin' to get shed of them otherwise, an' I can tell you for a fact In'ians fired up ain't the same by a long shot as In'ians settin' in the shade. Let 'em have all of it as far as I'm concerned. Better to do that an' live to rob another day than get shot in the back by a mob of the bastards chasin' us... Challo?'

The dark man turned in the direction of the arroyo, spoke almost as though for his own concern when he mildly said, 'I don't see no blanket.'

Marshal Boyle reponded to that. 'They

argue a lot when they're palaverin'. One of you gents got a canteen?'

The renegades ignored Marshal Boyle. He walked east a ways and flagged with his hat for Sears and Murphy to come in among the rocks.

That older renegade watched the pair of riders turn inward at a walk and spoke to the lawman. 'They got to get rid of them weapons.'

Boyle walked out to meet the blacksmith and his companion, told them to leave their guns behind and lead their horses. As they were doing this he told them all that had happened up to this point and the blacksmith wagged his head but said nothing. Jim Murphy spoke though. 'Whose side are we on now?' he asked.

The blacksmith tartly replied. 'Nobody's side, Jim. We're smack dab in the middle an' I'd guess our hides are about as likely to be hung on a fence by one bunch as the other.'

'Marshal, who's that dark feller?'

'All I know is that the others call him Challo.'

'In'ian or Mex?'

'I don't know, but he's got no accent.'

'Marshal, next time you want me to ride with you I'm goin' to be sick a-bed.'

One of the renegades around Challo abruptly gestured and spoke loudly. 'They're wavin' a blanket.'

Challo faced the lawman. 'Half the money an' they let us ride away without no trouble. *Quien sabe?*'

Boyle nodded and walked to his waiting horse. The heat was as bad as it would get. The sun was a malevolent misty orb directly overhead. The only shadows men cast now were underfoot.

Marshal Boyle rode toward the arroyo as he had done before, at a slow walk. When he got to the lip and halted Hugh Black gestured for him to ride down. As Boyle dismounted he said, 'My horse is bad off for water.'

Hugh Black spoke gutterally to a nearby 'breed who led the marshal's animal away. Black considered the larger man for a long moment, and Boyle's heart sank. If the Indian rejected the offer of half the money it would mean they would fight.

Black said, 'You had the whole amount?'

Boyle nodded.

'Any trouble gettin' it?'

'Some. The old screwt who runs the stages balked because of what you got from his safe.'

'But he come through?'

'Yes.'

'Marshal, we talked.'

Boyle spoke woodenly, 'An' decided not to take half.'

'Yes. It's pretty simple. We planned this for almost a year an' now we don't like the idea of bein' robbed by renegades.'

Boule said, 'I told 'em there was sixteen of you.'

Hugh Black's gaze showed faint irony. 'Bad enough that we raided your town an' get you in the middle, but worse to have renegades ambush you.'

Boyle watched an Indian swatting deer flies. 'That's why I didn't come alone. I figured somethin' like that might happen.'

'Why?'

'Well, for one thing, their spokesman, a

feller called Challo, as good as told me he'd been sent to rob me.'

'Who sent him?'

Boyle was slow to reply. 'A feller in town.'

Black's gaze did not waver. 'The fat storekeeper?'

Boyle nodded.

Black was momentarily silent, then he said, 'He was the one who had His Horse Is Black killed.'

Boyle shifted stance without answering. Hugh Black looked around as an Indian led up the lawman's horse. Without looking away from the large animal he said, 'Go back. Tell them they'll never leave them rocks alive.' Black faced around. 'How did Hammond get those renegades set for what they done?'

Marshal Boyle could only guess about that. 'He sent a telegram to someone over in Tonopah. My guess is that when he left town a few days back he went over there, arranged for the renegades to come over here, an' when they come he told them I'd be goin' up to your meadow, an' they bushwhacked me. That's mostly guesswork, but when I get back to town I'll wring the story out of Mister Hammond.'

That dour older Indian said something in a curt tone of voice to Hugh Black, who nodded and gestured for Marshal Boyle to mount his animal. When the lawman was astride Black said, 'You'n your friends get away from them rocks if you can. We'll be along.'

As Marshal Boyle rode in the direction of the rocks he saw that youngster with the crossed bullet belts standing on a rock watching. He did not like the idea of someone that young getting killed but after he got back into the boulder field Challo and three of his friends were waiting. The youngster was not among them.

Boyle swung down and said, 'No trade. They want all the money.'

The goat-eyed 'breed glowered. He asked if Challo wanted to die for some pouches of money and a renegade standing beside the goat-eyed man nodded his head.

Challo asked if they would be allowed to ride away and Boyle shrugged massive shoulders. 'They're fired up to fight,' he stated.

Another renegade 'breed, dripping sweat and angry-eyed, addressed Challo. 'Whoever sent you out here most likely knew them tomahawks would be waiting. Who was it, Challo?'

The swarthy man twisted from the waist to gaze in the direction of the arroyo. Heat-haze made the land undulate. He turned back, ignored the man who had asked who had set this up and said, 'All right. They can have the damned money, an' we'll go back to Martindale and clean out the town, the bank an' every other place they'll have money.' He glared at the marshal. 'Someone's got to pay and by gawd they will.'

He growled at the youngster to fetch the money pouches. While the lad was obeying Challo ignored Marshal Boyle to speak to his companions. 'We'll likely get more from the town anyway.'

The dour man jerked his thumb. 'What about him?'

Challo looked at the lawman. 'He helped

us. We leave him be.'

A renegade brought Boyle's animal. As he was mounting he saw the liveryman and the blacksmith being guarded by a burly 'breed. He spoke from the saddle to Challo. 'Let them go.'

Challo shook his head. 'There's another one. He was ridin' a muscled-up, pig-eyed horse.' He looked around. 'Find him,' he told the other renegades. Challo considered the large man on the large horse. 'Take them pouches. Tell them broncos we'll leave peaceably an' we expect them to keep their word now that they got the damned money.'

Marshal Boyle did not move. 'Let them fellers go. All they done was ride along with me.'

Challo shook his head. 'No! We take them with us. If any tomahawks come after us we'll kill them.'

Boyle dropped the little pouches. 'Take it to the In'ians yourself,' he said, and leaned to dismount.

The goat-eyed man spoke swiftly. 'Let 'em go, Challo. They ain't no good to us.

They'll just slow us down.'

Challo's expression was murderous as he and Marshal Boyle stared at each other. The old, dour renegade told the youngster to pick up the pouches and give them to the man on the big horse. As the youth was doing this the dour renegade addressed Challo. 'You ever seen what In'ians do to people? I have an' by gawd it's a sight that'll haunt you for the rest of your life. Let them fellers go. Send the marshal over yonder with the damned money an' let's get a-horseback. We've wasted more'n half the damned day talkin'!'

Challo considered his companions, their faces showed defiance. He looked up at the lawman. 'Go on. Make sure you get their word we can ride away without trouble. Go on, dammit!'

'As soon as I see them two friends of mine on their horses ridin' out of the rocks.'

Challo did not yell to the solitary guard, one of the other renegades did. He told the guard to allow the prisoners to mount up and be on their way.

He obeyed, but with bewilderment, and when Sears and Murphy were out of the rock field their guard came back where the others were standing, looking baffled.

The dour older renegade growled for him to keep his mouth shut, he obeyed but his bewilderment deepened. He and the others watched the marshal ride toward the distant arroyo. When he was mid-way Challo faced his companions. 'When he comes back we leave him dead in these damned rocks.'

The dour renegade spoke while watching the marshal ride. He said, 'He ain't comin' back an' if we don't do nothin' else we better get a-horseback right now an' ride for it.'

The renegade was right about one thing; after Marshal Boyle reached the arroyo and rode down into it and tossed the little pouches to the Indians then dismounted, loosened his cinch and addressed Hugh Black. 'They'll run for it. Let 'em go. You got your money.' Boyle faced around, the Indians were hefting the little pouches. The eldest among them asked the lawman if all the money was there. Boyle nodded.

One of the 'breeds said, 'We got to count it. Set in the shade, Marshal.'

It was good advice, but there was no shade in the arroyo. Hugh Black jerked his head and led the lawman clear of the others, who were emptying pouches and counting money. Black hunkered against the south wall of the gulch. When the marshal did the same Black said, 'You did it right.'

Boyle shrugged and mopped sweat. 'It's pretty near over as far as I'm concerned,' he said.

Black gazed at the large man. 'Let the renegades escape?'

'Sort of. Their spokesman said something about robbing the town. I got to round up the fellers who come with me an' get back as quick as I can.'

This discussion was broken by a gunshot. Everyone in the arroyo dropped what they'd been doing to go to the east side and peer out.

Over near the rock field two men were dragging a third man to safety among the boulders. They were excellent targets but whoever had shot the downed renegade did not fire again. Hugh Black said, 'You set up an ambush?'

Marshal Boyle shook his head. He was squinting for a sighting of burnt gunpowder and did not find any such indication of the location of the man who had fired. He shook sweat off and growled. 'Smitty, sure as hell, but where is he?'

The land shimmered under a pitiless sun but there was no movement. The marshal said, 'Scairt 'em. Now they won't leave the rocks. The damned fool. He should've let 'em go.'

An Indian came over to speak to Hugh Black in their native tongue. Black interrupted for the lawman. 'Your bush-whacker's among the rocks.'

Boyle scowled. 'What!'

'My friends saw him. He's around behind somewhere. They saw him slip from rock to rock after firing.'

Marshal Boyle eased back from the arroyo wall, and swore. Haldane was putting the blacksmith and the liveryman in a bad position. The renegades would probably assume one of them, in the act of leaving, had shot that renegade. He said, 'Damned fool. They'll go after the other two. They don't have much of a head start. They'll overtake 'em as sure as I'm standin' here.'

Hugh Black whistled and made a flinging high gesture with one arm. He brushed Boyle's arm. 'Let's see how good that prow-horse you ride is. We're goin' after whoever's in them rocks.'

As the lawman snugged his cinch and stepped across leather Hugh Black and his companions were already riding up out of the arroyo.

They were lithe, intense men carrying Winchesters in one hand, reins in the other hand. Black led them straight toward the forted-up renegades.

By the time Marshal Boyle emerged from the gully and rode after the Indians someone among the boulders began firing. At first it was just one man but by the time the Indians were mid-way at least two other renegades joined the fight.

The Indians did not fire until they were close enough to see an occasional head arise to lean down over gunsights in the rocks, then they not only fired but they howled.

Marshal Boyle stood in his stirrups seeking Murphy and Sears. He saw some distant dust but no riders. As he eased down he caught sight of sunlight off blue steel near the eastern-most edge of the boulder field. He saw the dirty grey puff when someone back there fired. Several renegades twisted to face this threat behind them and one of them emptied his saddle gun in that direction. Boyle saw the puffs as bullets struck rock. He did not see the shooter and did not expect to. For all he knew Smitty Haldane was a good coachman, but that was all he knew. How the whip had sneaked in to the boulder field undetected was something the lawman intended to ask, if he and Haldane ever met again.

From the south three hard-riding men raised dust and fired as they rode. The fact that they were coming from the direction

191

Sears and Murphy would have taken the marshal was sure who they would be. He was also aware that firing weapons from the hurricane deck of running horses wasted lead and made noise but accomplished little else.

The renegades had Indians in front, a sniper east of them and now three returning townsmen behind them.

Marshal Boyle felt a slight jerk and looked down. Someone's wild bullet had neatly torn the leather cap off his saddlehorn.

He veered away easterly. Without weapons he could not defend himself let alone participate in the fight, which had dust arising even among the boulders where desperate renegades constantly moved after firing.

The fight was furiously pressed by the renegades. They probably did not consider the consequences of surrendering. All they had time for was resistance and they fought like tigers.

They knew by now there were not sixteen Indians but that mattered less than the knowledge that they were under attack front and back with a sniper among the boulders with them.

Boyle heard a scream, looked back and saw the dour old renegade drop his carbine, grab his middle and tumble off a rock.

He noticed the gunfire was slackening among the rocks. Hugh Black rode his horse into the rock field with a high-held six-gun poised. There were several nearly simultaneous shots. Black went off his horse head first.

His companions howled and scrabbled among the rocks. Sears, and the liveryman who had been joined by Clancy, were at the southerly perimeter of the boulder field. They dismounted on the fly and hurled themselves toward the nearest shelter. A man called them from hiding. Smitty Haldane was out of ammunition. He snake-crawled to their protective boulders where they gave him ammunition for his hand-gun but they had none for his Winchester. He left the saddle gun and belly-crawled with the liveryman, the blacksmith, and the saloonkeeper.

The Indians were taking chances no one in their right mind would take and one of them, the raffish, dour, bronco was shot through the head. He dropped like a sack of wet grain. Two of his friends widened their manhunt, got north and south of the killer in his forted-up boulder position, arose and walked steadily toward his hiding place firing, levering up and firing. The renegade could not raise his head to return the fire until one of the Indians sprang atop a rock where the renegade was crouching and would have killed him but the renegade swung his six-gun before the Indian could position his carbine.

The crouching man did not fire but someone did; the second enfilading Indian fired pointblank from between two rocks.

The renegade was knocked against a rock at his back where he hung briefly, then toppled forward, dead.

Someone was yelling at the top of his voice that he gave up, that he had no ammunition and surrendered.

The fight was finished. A stalwart full-blood called for the surrendering renegade to stand up where he could be seen and raise his hands.

The renegade arose hands high, and the Indian shot him three times.

Marshal Boyle came through the boulders, left his horse, scooped up someone's six-gun, which was empty, ignored the calls of Haldane, Sears, Clancy and Murphy to make his way where Indians stood looking down.

Boyle sank to one knee. Hugh Black's face, head and shirt were bloody. He leaned over and using the tip of his forefinger traced the path of the bullet where it had mangled Hugh Black's left ear and had carved a gory gash from front to back above his temple. He looked up. 'You know how to make a travois?' he asked. Two Indians nodded.

'Make one, we got to get him to town.'

An Indian said, 'He's dead.'

'He ain't dead. Make somethin' to haul him on. *Move!*'

The Indian moved.

# 11

## The Ride Back

Among the renegades one survived. Smitty Haldane rousted him from hiding among the rocks. It was the youngster wearing crossed bandoleers, Mexican style.

He stood straight biting his lip. Haldane asked his name. The boy answered in an unsteady voice. 'Miguel Cardoza. You killed my brother.'

Smitty, the liveryman and saloonman took the only surviving renegade over where men were standing above Hugh Black. A solemn 'breed regarded the boy, raised his gaze to Smitty and said, 'Kill him.'

Marshal Boyle faced the 'breed. 'You touch him an' I'll break every bone in your body.'

The Indian did not relent but he was

facing a man six inches taller, easily fifty pounds heavier, all muscle and bone. He looked away.

The blacksmith stood beside the lad who was fighting hard not to cry.

Hugh Black's Indians were down to two survivors. When Marshal Boyle told the survivors they would go down to Martindale where Black could be cared for, the surviving two broncos went to find their dead companions, drag them toward a secluded place among huge rocks and without speaking went to work gathering rocks to be piled atop the corpses.

When the travois was ready and the animals had been caught, the lawman was ready to leave. The Indians were still piling rocks neither heeding the other survivors or speaking among themselves.

Andy Sears, who knew something about tribesmen jerked his head, led the others where the cairn was being erected and, like the Indians, went to work fetching rocks. The others including the marshal followed the blacksmith's example.

There was an abundance of rocks and

with everyone helping they finished making the cairn and went back to the travois, on which the Indians placed Hugh Black, sprang astride and as the cavalcade left the boulder field an Indian rode on each side of the travois.

Because of the dearth of timber the travois had been cobbled together from dead chaparral limbs which were not long enough so they had been spliced and bound tightly. It was a crude horsedrawn stretcher and Marshal Boyle twisted often in the saddle to be sure it was holding together when held to a walk by its rider.

Andy Sears had the captured boy on his left side. They did not converse, none of them did in fact, but Andy's occasional sidelong glance at the boy was compassionate if not altogether under- standing. Andy had never married, some- thing he hadn't regretted but he had always been fond of children, which was a good thing. The farther they got from the boulder field the less often the boy looked back.

They hadn't buried the renegades. Later, someone might come out from town and tend to that.

The heat was stifling, above the riders a malevolent sun was slightly off-centre. No one knew the time of day and no one cared about that.

They stopped once, when one of the Indians called in fractured English that Hugh Black was bleeding.

Marshal Boyle went back, was told by Clancy Harney the unconscious man needed a tighter bandage around his head. As Clancy fished forth a fairly clean blue bandana he looked around. An Indian offered his head band. Clancy ignored the sweaty, filthy offering and accepted two bandannas, one from Marshal Boyle, one from Smitty Haldane. He removed the soggy wrapping which had been improvised back at the boulder field, flung it aside, stanched the bleeding with one bandana, told the lawman to knot the other two, and made a wrapping that absorbed blood but which was tight enough not to slip nor encourage more bleeding. As Haldane straightened up he addressed the marshal. 'Get some water down him,' he said, and this was done by the simple expedient of holding Black's head up, opening his mouth and tipping a water-gut. He had to instinctively swallow or gag. He swallowed.

They resumed the ride with thirsty, worn-down saddle animals scuffing dust, plodding head-down and dripping sweat even from their belly hairs.

Clancy edged up beside Boyle and spoke softly. 'He ain't goin' to make it.'

Boyle scowled. 'He'll make it.'

Clancy asked where the pouches were and again the lawman replied curtly. 'Back in the arroyo I expect, an' right now I don't give a damn.'

Clancy dropped back to ride stirrup with Haldane. He did not mention the large man's brusqueness, he repeated what he had said about Hugh Black not arriving in Martindale alive and got a scoffing reply. 'I've seen 'em shot worse'n that an' they never stopped talkin'.'

There were blue-tailed flies on Black's clothing and circling *sopolites* overhead.

Marshal Boyle watched them and wondered for about the hundredth time in his life if buzzards could smell blood from the sky, or whether they somehow sensed when there was a possible meal for them down below.

Andy Sear's young riding partner finally cried. He bent over the saddle swell trying as hard as he could to master the tears and the sobs. Andy reached over gently and patted the boy's shoulder. He did not say a word. None of them did. Except for the blacksmith none of the others acted as though they heard the gut-wrenching sobs.

They had Martindale's roofs in sight before their animals perked up and lengthened their stride, the scent of water carried a fair distance even when the sun was blazing.

As they rode down Main Street townsmen came out to stand like statues and watch. Marshal Boyle told the liveryman and Smitty Haldane to take care of the animals. He and the pair of Indians carried Hugh Black into the jailhouse where it was ten degrees cooler, put him on a bunk in a cell and the lawman sent Clancy for the minister.

There was no doctor in Martindale. The nearest medical man was a day's ride north. Reverend Severn had, over the years, been summoned for sickness and broken bones. He had become proficient because he'd had to.

They removed the bandage, washed the injured man's face with cold water and got a little whiskey down him from the marshal's bottle in the desk. It heightened Black's colour but he did not open his eyes and his breathing remained ragged. One of the Indians did an odd thing—for an Indian—he leaned over and made the sign of the cross on Hugh Black's chest.

The preacher arrived carrying a small leather satchel. He did not ask how the wounded man had been injured, in fact he said nothing at all as he dampened the bandage before removing it, and afterwards sucked in a breath as he examined the injury.

He asked for clean cloth. Andy Sears took the lad with him over to the emporium, got some clean linen from the wide-eyed clerk who had never before seen a youngster wearing crossed bandoleers with bullets in most of the loops. Andy paid and led the way back across the road without a word to either the clerk or to his shadow, Miguel Cardoza.

Enoch Severn cleansed the wound, staunched what little blood still trickled, and sprinkled some powder over the injury. It must have stung because Hugh Black flinched. Severn looked up at the lawman. 'Good sign. He can feel.'

Marshal Boyle returned to his office, stood by the small barred window gazing across the road where people were entering and departing from the general store.

He was still standing there when Clancy spoke from behind him. 'What about the money, Marshal?'

Boyle turned. 'You want to go get it?'

The saloonman, tired all the way through, dry as cotton and with sore thighs because he rarely rode a horse, considered the large man in silence for a moment then shook his head.

Marshal Boyle made a tight, humourless smile. 'I didn't think so. I'll go back for it in the morning.'

'What about them two In'ians?'

'What about them?'

'That's our money. They done the same as holdin' us up at gunpoint.'

Marshal Boyle went to his desk, sat down, groaned and leaned back to say, 'It ain't the In'ians, Clancy. We'd have made a trade with 'em an' they'd have left. It was those sons of bitching renegades.'

'They're dead, Marshal.'

'For a fact, but they didn't just happen to be out there, Clancy.'

The saloonman went to the door. 'I got a business to run.'

Marshal Boyle nodded after the saloonman. Everybody had a business to run, and one first-rate son of a bitch in Martindale also had a sideline to his storekeeping business.

Enoch Severn appeared in the cell-room doorway. His sleeves were rolled up to the elbows, his hands had blood on them. He said, 'He came around.

Oh, he'll make it if that's what's worryin' you. I'd guess that by tomorrow he'll be talkin'. But he's goin' to have as bad a headache as a man can get.' The preacher stepped to the desk and dropped some white pills on it. 'Give him two of those things a couple of times a day. They won't cure the headache but it'll hold off the pain for several hours.' Severn went to the door, looked back and asked a question. 'You brought the money back with you?'

Boyle shook hes head. 'It's still up there. I'll go up in the morning and bring it back.'

The minister faintly frowned. 'It'll still be there?'

'I think so. Enoch, it wasn't the money. Some men died up there and Hugh Black needed to be brought to town right away.'

Severn nodded. 'A human life doesn't have a cash value. I understand.'

After the minister left Marshal Boyle returned to the window. At the store people were still coming and going, but not as many as an hour before.

He went down to the cell room. The Indians were gone but the blacksmith and the youngster were in the cell. Boyle asked about the Indians. Sears said they had talked in some Indian language and had departed. He jutted his jaw in the direction of the man on the cot who was watching Marshal Boyle from bloodshot eyes. Boyle filled a cup from a pitcher, handed it and two pills to Hugh Black. The Indian grimaced over the pills and drained the cup.

Andy Sears said, 'He talked to them In'ians before they left.'

As Marshal Boyle pulled up a three-legged stool and sat at the bedside, the blacksmith said if he wasn't needed he'd like to go over to the store and buy the lad some decent clothes.

Marshal Boyle looked at the lad, who looked stoically back. 'Andy, get those bandoleers off him.'

After Sears and Miguel Cardoza left, Marshal Boyle met the bloodshot gaze of Hugh Black, and gently wagged his head. 'First time in my life,' he told the other man, 'I ever got caught in the middle like up yonder.'

'You did right,' the Indian said. 'Do you have some whiskey?'

Boyle considered. He had whiskey but instinct warned him about giving any to the man on top of those big white pills. He said, 'Give 'em time. Reverend Severn said they'd stop the headache.'

Hugh Black considered the large man stoically. 'When?'

Boyle had no idea but he made a guess. 'Maybe half an hour, if they ain't worked by then I'll get the whiskey. You sent the In'ians away?'

'Yes. Do you know which one of those renegades shot me?'

'No, an' it don't matter. They're all dead. Are your tomahawks comin' back?'

'To this place? No. Not ever.'

'You sent 'em back where they come from?'

'Yes, but first they go up yonder an' get the pouches. Then they head for home.'

Marshal Boyle sat a long moment in silence. He hadn't looked forward to returning to the rock field and the arroyo. Now he wouldn't have to, but there would be questions about the money. He leaned with both big hands clasped between his knees when he said, 'I figured they might have brought the pouches down here with 'em.'

Hugh Black eyed the large man. 'You don't understand tomahawks, Marshal. They don't care about that money except that it's the reason we came here, an' they got to take it back to prove what they did. But for itself...' Hugh Black very carefully shook his head.

The lawman changed the subject. 'That's a nasty sideswipe you got.'

Black replied quietly, 'They told me you had the stretcher made an' struck out to get me down here. I owe you, Marshal.'

Boyle grinned. 'The money, Mister Black?'

The Indian did not grin back but he said, 'In'ians go on an honour trip. In my case for the spirit of His Horse Is Black. Marshal, the tribesmen need that money, the gov'ment don't care for 'em, don't like In'ians. In'ian agents and commissioners sell allotments of beef to townsmen, Indians eat rabbits and rats. President Grant's brother got rich selling In'ian beef allotments. The money will help. I can't give it back.'

Marshal Boyle regarded the younger man with the bandaged head. 'Did the government send you to school?'

'Not the government. I went to a Catholic mission school. In'ians are doing that now.' Hugh Black'e eyes mirrored humour. 'You educate us an' see what happens?'

Marshal Boyle made a small, rueful smile. He had pondered about this some time back and ended up blaming schools on reservations for producing men like Hugh Black. He said, 'It ain't that we owe you. What happened before you was born an' mostly before I was born, was done by other whites. Mostly, they're dead now. You can't get revenge on them an' the rest of us didn't have a damned thing to do with what happened back then.'

Hugh Black's eyes were fixed on the

209

lawman. 'You make a good excuse. Now tell me, what about the white man who sent those renegades to take our money from you?'

Marshal Boyle had no answer. Maybe he should have anticipated that remark but he hadn't. Hugh Black was subtle. Arnold Boyle was as subtle as a rock slide. He slapped his legs and arose. 'I'll fetch the whiskey. How's your headache?'

'It's gone,' Black stated, then hurriedly also said, 'But I got other aches.'

Marshal Boyle went up front to rummage for his bottle. Andy Sears walked in with Miguel Cardoza. Boyle stood behind the desk staring. Andy said, 'We even got him a shearing and an all-over bath at the tonsorial parlour.'

The youth smiled slightly at the formidable large man with the badge and raised one trouser leg to show new boots. The marshal admired the boots effusively, Miguel Cardoza smiled from ear to ear. As the boy was lowering the trouser leg Marshal Boyle looked at the blacksmith, who looked back as he said, 'When he's bigger I'll teach him a trade. Right now he's got to go to the schoolhouse. He can read a tad but can't hardly write.'

Marshal Boyle said nothing as he continued to regard the blacksmith. Andy cleared his throat, 'A man should have a son, Marshal.'

Boyle nodded. 'That's a fact.' He smiled at Miguel Cardoza. 'Come visit me. I don't have no youngster either. All right?'

The youth gravely inclined his head. His image of the large man had been formed in the rock field.

When Boyle got back to the cell Hugh Black had managed to prop himself up. He said, 'Those are magic pills. I feel as good as I ever did.' Black took the bottle, tipped it, swallowed several times and for the few additional minutes the marshal spent with him, his eyes sparkled, his colour was good and only when he began running words together and slurring them did Marshal Boyle leave.

He went up to Clancy's place where the rawboned shockle-headed substitute barman told him Clancy had lolled in a hot bath, had afterwards taken two jolts of malt whiskey and was now asleep on the cot in the storeroom snoring like buffalo stuck in the mud.

The day was wearing along. There were shadows on the west side of the roadway when he went down to the emporium. He didn't learn much there either. Mister Hammond had not been to the store all day and the clerk had no idea where he was.

Marshal Boyle had an early supper, which meant except for the gossipy caféman there were only four other men at the counter. Two were cowmen who had come in for supplies and the mail. They could not have avoided hearing the main topic in Martindale, but being naturally discreet men they nodded to the lawman, asked no questions, finished their meals in silence, paid up and departed.

Old Jake Miller was hunched at the counter and glared at Marshal Boyle from jaundiced eyes. He too had heard about the trouble up north. The other diner was old Abner Holt, who rarely had money for a café-cooked meal. He did not nod nor in any other way indicate that he had seen the lawman enter.

Jake waited until the caféman was in his kitchen rustling up Boyle's supper before he said, 'You lost the money? That's what folks are sayin'. You got in a fight up yonder an' lost the money.'

Marshal Boyle leaned back when the caféman brought his platter, ignored the old stager and went to work with his knife and fork.

Jake got as red as a beet. 'You gone deef? I said folks are sayin'...'

Boyle put down his implements. 'You didn't get burnt out, did you? You wasn't around when we rode up there, was you? Jake, you're a real pain in the ass. Have been since I've known you. I did my best with the money.'

'You brought back that subbitching 'breed In'ian that held up the town. You figure to hang him?'

Marshal Boyle twisted on the bench. The caféman took root behind the counter. He had seen the marshal angry before.

Boyle poked the stager in the chest with a stiff, large finger, nearly punching him off the bench. As Jake squawked Boyle said, 'Why did you paint that old bronco's tombstone?'

'I done no such thing! That was some boys.'

'You knew that? How much did you pay them?'

'I had nothin' to do with that. It was Hammond paid 'em.'

'How do you know that?'

'Because one's the son of my yardman. The boy showed his paw the money an' told him how he'd got it. Now then, you punch me again an' I'll—I'll figure somethin'. You can't go around bullyin' folks. I'll take it up with the town council.'

Marshal Boyle went back to his meal. By the time he had finished only Abner Holt was still at the counter, and he arose, dropped silver coins beside his plate and as he turned to depart he winked.

Marshal Boyle winked back.

# 12

## 'Coffee, Lots of Coffee!'

It bothered the marshal when Mister Hammond did not arrive at the store, something which mystified his clerk as it did the lawman. The clerk said, 'He hardly ever leaves and stays away.'

As he had done before the marshal went over to the corralyard. Also, as before, old Jake was short with him. He said he knew for a fact that Mister Hammond hadn't gone anywhere on a stage, which the marshal had to accept for the simple reason that no one was in a better position to have that knowledge.

Jake looked malevolently at the lawman. 'You're interested? Last time you was in here you asked the same question. I told you then an' I'm tellin' you now—Mister Hammond never rode a stage out of here the last few days. Go talk to Jim at the livery barn. Maybe Mister Hammond went a-horseback.'

This is exactly what the marshal did. It was also what he'd intended to do after visiting old Jake. But Jim Murphy was not much more help than Jake had been. He hadn't even seen the storekeeper lately and he certainly had not hired out a rig or an animal to him.

Boyle knew where Mister Hammond lived, in one of the only two-storeyed homes in Martindale. He didn't go to the house, he went down a back alley to the gate leading into the Hammond yard, entered and went to a shed that was two-thirds full of grass hay and smelled good. The blood-bay sorrel horse was not there. Neither was the saddle, blanket or bridle.

Boyle returned to the alley and was closing the gate when he heard a cat howling. He went up the alley until he found three boys who had chased a cat up an apple tree and were now down below throwing rocks at the frightened

216

cat. They were so engrossed in what they were doing they did not see nor hear the marshal until he caught the eldest boy by the scruff of the neck and flung him against the board fence. The other two boys whirled. They would have fled but it was too late. Marshal Boyle caught each of them by the shirt, hauled back then slammed them into each other, hard. One boy fell, the other one struggled and cried. Boyle pushed him away as he said, 'How old are you?'

'Thirteen, Mister Boyle.'

The marshal sneered. 'A thirteen-year-old cry baby. Next time I hear of any of you torturin' animals I'm goin' to lock you up and whale the daylights out of your pa. You understand me?'

Only two of the lads replied, the one who had been hurled into the fence was sitting on the ground rubbing his eyes. The two who spoke promised in terror never to be mean to an animal again.

There was an excellent possibility that they wouldn't, not because they wouldn't recover from being caught, but because if the marshal came for their fathers someone would find out why, and that could lead to another shellacking.

As the boys scattered Marshal Boyle continued up the alley to Main Street and crossed to his jailhouse. He was in there very briefly before going out back and saddling an animal. He left town riding north. He paused briefly at the minister's place to hand over the key to the jailhouse then loped for two miles northward.

If it was true thirsty animals could scent water over great distances, then it could also be true that lawmen could scent trouble—and storekeepers could scent abandoned money pouches.

It was not particularly hot when he left town but before he had he read shod-horse sign nearly as far as the boulder field, the sun was bearing down with heat and distances were beginning to dance and shimmer.

He did not have his Winchester, had not expected to need it. He passed the boulder field a half-mile to the west, but even that much distance was too close for the large, clumsy bird who flapped in an ungainly way out of the rock field.

The tracks headed toward the closest arroyo. How Mister Hammond knew the money had been left behind after the boulder-field fight was anyone's guess. Maybe he could indeed scent money the way buzzards scented-up dead rabbits, coyotes, lizards and snakes.

The marshal rarely indulged in fantasies and he did not now. He had no reason to think the storekeeper had known the money had been left behind after the rock-field fight, except that several people knew that it had which anyone of Mister Hammond's duplicitous tendencies could have found out, and that could very well account for the storekeeper's departure, and the fresh shod-horse marks Marshal Boyle had been following.

He did encounter two other sets of tracks, both of barefoot horses. They would belong to the Indians Hugh Black had sent to find the money. But their tracks were older than the shod-horse tracks.

The marshal alternately watched the sign

and scanned the countryside. As soon as he approached the expanse of treeless and brushless land in the vicinity of the arroyo, he studied the land more and the tracks less.

Somewhere ahead the shod-horse sign dipped into the arroyo. Marshal Boyle followed almost stoically until he reined to a halt on the lip of the gully. Below was an abundance of sign that a solitary rider had made a search. Boyle sat up there reading meaning into the tracks. The storekeeper had found the pouches, there was no doubt about that. He had moved tirelessly from side to side and from west to south. His tracks overlay earlier moccasin tracks. The impression Marshal Boyle got from the sign was that the storekeeper's search had been frantic and hasty. He would not have known the Indians were coming to find the same pouches, but something had kept him moving swiftly.

Boyle dismounted, used horse shade to protect him as he hunkered down. The shod-horse marks went easterly through the depths of the canyon. Boyle arose, mounted, scanned his back trail, saw nothing and eased the big animal downward then eastward following the storekeeper's tracks.

The heat had been steadily increasing for some time, but down in the gully it was worse. Boyle mopped sweat, tipped his hat low and squinted his eyes nearly closed. The heat did not exclusively bother two-legged things. Boyle's big horse plodded past a thornpin thicket without noticing the diamond back until it was beyond and the snake rattled. Boyle looked for it, or a companion if it had one, but could locate nothing. Snakes hid from hot sunlight. The base of flourishing bushes was a favourite place.

He came upon a little spring, which was a surprise, and watered his horse, drank his fill and easily read the sign here indicating that the storekeeper had dawdled, probably because he was unaccustomed to heat and glare.

The atmosphere was mildly muggy, waves of heat shimmered, animals with good sense hid out this time of any summer day in Nevada, but the two-legged variety was an exception. Marshal Boyle heard the gunshot. It sounded almost dull but it was unmistakably a gunshot. How far ahead he had no idea, the echo had sounded almost muffled.

He rode up a path to the north rim of the arroyo, saw no movement, no familiar shapes, and continued riding eastward up there where an occasional hot breeze blew which copious sweating made the little breeze seem helpful when it dried perspiration on man and horse.

Marshal Boyle rode with eyes squinted nearly closed. Eventually, he saw a loose horse coming his way. It had stepped on both reins, they had been torn off about a foot from the bridle.

The horse did not move fast, it trotted. There was too much heat for a faster gait.

Boyle had no difficulty catching the animal, in fact it changed course and came right up to him.

He knew the animal, removed its bridle, hung it from the horn, loosened the cinch and pointed the animal southward in the direction of Martindale.

He did not get back astride, he led his horse. A large man atop a large horse made an excellent target.

He was a few yards north of the arroyo when his horse abruptly threw up its head. There was nothing to tie the horse to so he hobbled it with his reins and went toward the edge of the arroyo.

Two horses standing head-hung from heat warp were standing together. In front of one horse was a dead Indian lying face up. He had been shot through the centre of the chest.

Boyle got belly down hoping heat waves would provide some concealment while he studied the arroyo and his surroundings. He saw nothing but he faintly heard a running horse going eastward. As he was leaning to arise he heard another distant gunshot, stood up, dusted off and shook his head. Anyone who would run a horse under these circumstances was begging to end up on foot.

He went back, freed his animal and led it. There was a third gunshot which the lawman fixed for direction and veered slightly northward of the arroyo which was beginning to rise toward open country.

When he saw another horse, standing wide-legged head down on the verge of collapsing he tied his own animal to a thicket, started walking with his six-gun in his fist and saw an Indian behind a yellowish boulder aiming his carbine. Boyle did not see what he was aiming at until there was another gunshot. The bullet broke pieces off the Indian's yellow rock and he ducked down behind it.

The Indian's back was to the lawman. Also, he was on the south side of the arroyo, but the invisible man who had shot at him was on the north side and saw Marshal Boyle. He yelled. 'It's me, Arthur Hammond. There's an In'ian behind that yellow rock.'

The shouting brought the Indian around in a frantic crouch.

Marshal Boyle signalled for him to stay down and continued walking. Again the storekeeper yelled. 'Marshal! He's behind you!'

Boyle neither stopped walking nor called back. He knew where Hammond was from his voice and did not alter course until he had to, then he halted facing a shallow gully and scarcely raised his voice. 'Stand up, Mister Hammond.'

'There's a damned tomahawk behind that yeller rock across the arroyo!'

'I know that,' Boyle said, still not raising his voice. 'Stand up. He's not goin' to fire again. *Stand up!*'

The storekeeper did not show himself but the next time he called he did not shout. 'There was two of 'em. I got one back aways. I'm not goin' to stand up while he's over yonder behind that rock!'

Marshal Boyle moved without haste to the shallow place where the storekeeper was lying. They saw each other at about the same time. Boyle was struck by the red, flushed face of the storekeeper. His clothing was soaked with sweat, it dripped from his chin as he looked up while clutching a Winchester saddle gun. 'He'll shoot you, Marshal. For Chris'sake get down.'

Boyle had known the storekeeper for years. This was the first time he'd ever seen him a-horseback so far from town. Mister Hammond, like the Martindale banker, was totally sedentary and right now he looked like a boiled lobster with frightened eyes and an unsteady mouth.

Marshal Boyle ignored the Indian across the arroyo. He hunkered down. 'Where's the pouches, Mister Hammond?'

The storekeeper's eyes widened. 'There is a damned In'ian across the gully an' as sure as I'm hid from him he's goin' to shoot you in the back.'

'Mister Hammond—where are the money pouches?'

'In the bags on my saddle. For Chris'sake forget the money. Shoot that tomahawk before he shoots you.'

Marshal Boyle stood and turned. 'The money pouches are in his saddle-bags.'

The Indian showed head and shoulders. He had his carbine in both hands.

Boyle called to him again. 'Take the pouches and go. Get the hell out of the country. *Go on, do it!*'

226

Arthur Hammond squawked and started to edge out of his shallow place. Marshal Boyle raised a boot, waited, then lowered it atop the storekeeper's hand, and leaned. 'Let go the gun,' he growled. Hammond pulled his hand free and glared upwards. 'Are you crazy? That money belongs to folks in town. I got it to take back an' give it to the fellers who put it up. Kill that damned In'ian! Don't let him take it!'

The marshal shifted his foot, leaned, caught hold of the storekeeper's Winchester and wrenched it free. He flung it behind and leaned for the hand-gun.

Hammond sucked back, his breath was coming in rattling gasps. He raised the six-gun. Marshal Boyle aimed a big boot and kicked, the gun sailed away and Hammond was rolled sideways by the impact. He rolled over and leaned to arise, hung there for several seconds, then collapsed face down.

Boyle went back to the arroyo on the north side and called to the Indian. 'Take his saddle-bags. You can count the pouches later. Strip his horse, turn it loose. It'll go

227

back to that little spring. Where's your horse?'

The Indian regarded the lawman with equal parts of wariness and wonderment. He said his horse was back a mile tied to a bush.

'Don't push the horse, but don't waste a lot of time getting away from here.'

The Indian freed the saddle-bags and flung them over his shoulder as he called to the large man above. 'Is Hugh Black dead?'

'No, he ain't dead an' he ain't goin' to die, but it'll be a while before he can set a horse.'

'You lock him up, huh?'

'No, I'm not goin' to lock him up, except to keep folks from hangin' him. As soon as he's fit to travel I'll put him on a stage out of our Territory.'

The Indian said, 'What about the fat man?'

'He's dead. Too much heat, too much sweatin' an' maybe too much being scairt.'

'You leave him here?'

'No, my horse'll carry double. Now go

228

find your horse an' get the hell out of the country.'

The Indian scrambled out of the arroyo and loped westerly as though the saddle-bags were weightless. Only once did he look back but the large lawman was out of his sight.

Getting Mister Hammond shoved behind the cantle of his big horse and tying him could not have been accomplished by a smaller or less powerful man. Even then Marshal Boyle leaned on the horse for a long moment before mounting and starting for Martindale.

His horse handled the large man who rode it and the dead fat man behind the saddle as though the additional weight did not matter, which it didn't; the big horse knew in which direction he was being ridden, which to him made all the difference.

Marshal Boyle did not reach town until dusk when most people were at supper. He carried Arthur Hammond to the front of his store and propped him there. He visited Hugh Black who was hungry so the lawman went over the café, which was empty except for the proprietor who was reading a newspaper with glasses half down his nose.

Marshal Boyle said he wanted four buckets, two of black java and two of stew. As he was recrossing the road the caféman watched from a window wondering who the marshal's second prisoner was.

While they ate in Hugh Black's cell Boyle told his guest exactly what had happened since he'd left town earlier. Black emptied the coffee pail and although his head had been rebandaged and was obviously swollen, he seemed not to be in pain. His appetite was good. He finished eating long before the marshal did, and he asked questions which Boyle answered forthrightly. The foremost question had to do with why the marshal had allowed the surviving Indian to take the saddlebags, which Boyle also answered forthrightly.

'That was the agreement.'

Black studied the large man, seemed about to speak then didn't, but nodded as though he understood. He told Boyle about the preacher returning to re-dress the wound. He also said that according to Reverend Severn he would be able to ride within a week, to which Marshal Boyle said, 'Be better if you left tomorrow or the next day. Not on horseback, in a coach. There'll be lynch-talk, Mister Black. Can you ride a stage?'

'Yes. What will they say if you let me go?'

The big man shrugged. 'Whatever they want to, I expect, but not to my face. To save Martindale they agreed to pay you, which was done. I expect it's natural when the danger is past for folks to think of a dozen ways they would have done it better.'

Boyle picked up the empty pails, said, 'No headache?'

'Not unless I shake my head.'

At the cell doorway the lawman said, 'Sleep good. In the morning I'll put you on the southbound stage. It leaves about sun-up. I'll come for you.'

When full night was down Preacher

231

Severn came to the jailhouse. He had been told about the dead man propped in front of the door across the road. Boyle told him only that Mister Hammond must have died of sunstroke. He'd found him and brought him back to town. The minister had no difficulty believing that, in fact he said, 'I warned him he was too heavy, that his heart would likely give out one of these days.'

Marshal Boyle nodded woodenly.

'How is your prisoner?' Severn asked.

'Sleepin' like a log. I fed him. He said he don't hurt much unless he moves his head.'

'If he's sleepin' I won't bother him. Marshal, about those things In'ians hung on the tombstone...it's real close to the gate into the cemetery. I'm not sure they should be left there. Folks comin' to visit other graves—that's the first thing they see.'

'They complained?' asked the lawman.

'No. But—'

'Leave 'em be, Reverend. That tombstone might remind folks someday that except for that tombstone there wouldn't be a town here.'

Severn nodded and went to the door. 'I'll look in on Hugh Black tomorrow,' he said before departing.

Marshal Boyle nodded woodenly again.

Before bedding down he went to Jake Miller's office at the corralyard, ascertained from a Mexican yardman the morning stage would leave about five, about sun-up, then went on to the boarding-house.

He got about five hours' sleep, was booted and hatted well before sunrise, collected Hugh Black, took him to the corralyard, paid for his ride south and was watching the coach leave town at the lower end when Jake Miller returned from the café sucking his teeth. He stopped at sight of the marshal in his gateway, spat once and said, 'You're up early. Goin' out to smell the flowers are you?'

Boyle considered the disagreeable old man through a moment of quiet, then slowly drew and cocked his six-gun. Old Jake lost all colour, his knees trembled as the lawman raised the gun with the barrel

233

no more than a foot from Jake's face. Jake croaked, 'I was just joshin', I didn't mean no harm.'

'You never joshed in your misspent life that you didn't mean harm,' Boyle said, pushing the barrel closer. 'Jake, if I hear about you complainin' about how I do my job one more time, I'll kill you. You understand what I said?'

'I understand, Marshal. Believe me, we never had a better lawman since I been in Martindale. Never. Not a single one...what happened to Mister Hammond, down in front of his store stiff as a ramrod.'

'His heart quit yestiddy from the heat. I expect you'll make up stories about that.'

'No sir, on my oath I won't do no such a thing.'

'An' what about tellin' folks I didn't handle them In'ians right?'

'You done exactly right. No one could've done any better. You most likely saved the town.'

'An' you'll say you was glad to help buy 'em off?'

'I was glad to. I give you my word,

Mister Boyle, I was real glad to.'

Boyle leathered the six-gun, brushed past the frightened stager and headed for the first lighted window the full length of Main Street.

When he walked in the caféman looked startled. He had never fed the town marshal before seven o'clock.

Boyle sat down, both hands locked atop the counter and said, 'Whatever you got that's fit to eat an' coffee. Lots of coffee.'